Lillianna smiled at Thomas. "Hmm… maybe there's hope for you yet."

"I wouldn't hold my breath."

"No, you wouldn't."

"Ouch, that wasn't nice."

Lillianna sighed. "What am I going to do with you?"

"Marry me, hopefully?"

"I'm not ready yet, Thomas."

"Why?"

"Well, because. There are just so many things that we need to work through first. We don't believe the same things. I…I'm just not ready. If I marry, I need total peace about it."

"Will you please wait for me, then?"

"Of course. I already told you I would. Do you doubt my word?"

He shook his head. "Just worried, I guess. A lot could happen in a year. We'll be so far apart."

"Tommy, I can't imagine marrying anyone but you."

He bent down and looked deep into her eyes. "Nor I, you…"

By the grace of God, **J.E.B. Spredemann** resides in beautiful Southern Indiana Amish country and writes Christian fiction. May these books uplift you, inspire you, make you laugh and touch your heart. The author can be contacted via email at jebspredemann@gmail.com.

A SECRET
OF THE HEART

J.E.B. Spredemann

Recycling programs
for this product may
not exist in your area.

ISBN-13: 978-1-335-45576-5

A Secret of the Heart

Printed in U.S.A.

Author Note

It should be noted that the Amish people and their communities differ one from another. There are, in fact, no two Amish communities exactly alike. It is this premise on which this book is written. We have taken cautious steps to assure the authenticity of Amish practices and customs. Both Old Order Amish and New Order Amish are portrayed in this work of fiction and may be inconsistent with some Amish communities.

We, as *Englischers*, can learn a lot from the Plain People and their simple way of life. Their hard work, close-knit family life, and concern for others are to be applauded. As the Lord wills, may this special culture continue to be respected and remain so for many centuries to come, and may the light of God's salvation reach their hearts.

Unofficial Glossary
of Pennsylvania Dutch Words

Ach—Oh
Boppli—Baby
Bopplin—Babies
Brieder—Brothers
Bruder—Brother
Dat, Daed—Dad
Dawdi—Grandfather
Denki—Thanks
Der Herr—The Lord
Dochder—Daughter
Dummkopp—Dummy
Englischer—A non-Amish person
Ferhoodled—Mixed up, Crazy
Fraa—Woman, Wife
Gott—God
Gut—Good
Haus—House
Hiya—Hi
Hullo—Hello
Jah—Yes
Kapp—Prayer Covering
Lieb—Love
Mamm—Mom
Nee—No
Ordnung—Rules of the Amish Community
Rumspringa—Running around years
Schweschder—Sister
Schweschdern—Sisters
Vadder—Father
Wilkom—Welcome
Wunderbaar—Wonderful

Chapter One

Lillianna's eyes brightened as Carolanne approached her near the back door of Carolanne's folks' home. Carolanne's blue eyes reflected the cobalt of her newly-sewn cape dress.

"I can't believe you're married now!" Lillianna embraced her friend.

"I know. Isn't Samuel the handsomest *bu* you've ever seen?" Carolanne positively glowed.

Lillianna searched the room full of guests, mostly from their church district, to locate Carolanne's husband of one hour. Her gaze surveyed his well-defined physique, obvious to anyone, even through his blue button-down and suspenders, and landed on his seemingly happy countenance.

Was there more to Samuel Beachy than what met the eye? Lillianna was certain of it. Why would this man just show up out of the blue to snatch away her best friend? Of course, she knew that Carolanne had been corresponding by letter with him over the last year and that they'd enjoyed a few buggy rides together last fall. But that didn't explain his sudden reappearance. It was almost as though he were running away from something...or someone?

Lillianna dismissed her suspicions and brought her attention back to Carolanne. She wouldn't voice her concerns again. Carolanne was a grown woman capable of making her own intelligent choices.

Samuel turned and motioned for Carolanne to come near.

Carolanne squeezed Lillianna's hand. "Well, I better go. Seems Samuel wants to introduce me to someone."

Lillianna returned her friend's smile and watched as Carolanne flittered off to be by her husband's side.

Lillianna stepped outside the building for a breath of fresh air.

"Hey, Lillianna."

Lillianna turned and offered a brief smile to Marcus Yoder.

"You comin' to the gatherin' tonight after supper?"

Lillianna shook her head. "I don't think so, Marcus."

Marcus didn't mask his disappointment well. "Oh. Why not?"

It seemed like he'd been interested in Lillianna for a few months now. This wasn't the first time he'd shown his interest. "I'm feeling a little tired."

"I could give you a ride home," Marcus offered.

"Uh, no." Lillianna scanned the area, desperate for an acceptable excuse. She spotted the buggies parked out in the field. "I appreciate the offer, but I need to drive my own buggy home."

Marcus scratched his head as though thinking of a way he could spend more time with her.

"I'll see you later, Marcus." Lillianna abruptly walked away before he suggested something else. If she allowed him to, Marcus would jabber on for who knows how long. Lillianna glanced back to be certain her wannabe suitor hadn't followed, and released a relieved sigh when Marcus was sighted walking back into the house.

How am I going to get him to realize I'm not interested? She thought after two rejections that Marcus would get the hint, but no. He persisted. Lillianna couldn't find a good reason to not like him. He was nice enough and not too bad for looking.

He just wasn't…well, he wasn't *Tommy.*

Thomas Girod. Lillianna hadn't seen him in a long time, not since her family had moved away from Pennsylvania seven years ago. In their Amish district, the boys and girls were discouraged from playing together, but it hadn't stopped Thomas and Lillianna.

Lillianna closed her eyes, recalling the many Saturday afternoons they'd spent fishing at the stream just beyond her childhood home. Fishing was a good excuse to see her neighbor Thomas, who had quickly become her best friend, in spite of the fact that he was a boy and three years her senior.

"Don't forget me, Lil," Tommy said as he placed a kiss smack dab on her lips.

Lillianna's cheeks flushed furiously. "Thomas Girod, you...you kissed me?" Lillianna always thought Tommy would give her her first kiss some-day. But now? At twelve years old? This was totally unexpected.

"I mean it, Lil. Don't forget me." Thomas reached up and moved a strand of hair that had fallen onto her forehead. "Ever."

She'd never seen Tommy this serious. He really would miss her when her family moved away. "I won't," she promised.

Thomas settled back onto the rock he'd been fish-ing from and picked up his pole again. They contin-ued fishing as though the kiss had never happened, as though their lives weren't forever changed from that moment on.

That was the last time they'd ever gone to the stream together, and Lillianna had never forgotten Thomas or his kiss. She'd give anything to see or hear from Tommy now. The last two letters she'd written to him, nearly three years ago, had been re-turned to her marked "Return to Sender". She often wondered where he was, and what he was doing. Did he still live in Pennsylvania? Had he gotten married? Was he still alive? Lillianna hated to consider the an-tithesis to that last possibility.

When Lillianna opened her eyes, she realized the horse had already pulled into her driveway. Had she really been daydreaming that long? She chided herself for not paying better attention to the road. It was a good thing Sunshine was well-trained. *Dat* would have scolded her for certain, if he knew.

I miss you, Tommy, wherever you are.

"Lilly, aren't you going back over to Carolanne's for the gathering?" Judith Zook called to her daughter from the kitchen.

Lillianna frowned. "*Nee, Mamm.* I'm working on my quilt." She leaned over the quilting frame and weaved a few more stitches into the colorful fabric.

"Would you like some help? My fingers are just aching to do some quilting."

Lillianna smiled. "Be my guest."

"It wonders me why you're not joining the young folks. Seems to me like it would be a *gut* opportunity to meet some new friends."

"I know. It's just that… *Mamm*, have you heard any news lately from our friends in Pennsylvania?" Lillianna attempted not to sound too obvious. "I often wonder how everyone is doing over in Bishop Mast's district."

Judith shook her head. "Haven't heard much since that accident the Girods had a few years back."

Lillianna's pulse quickened. "Accident? I never heard about an accident. What happened?"

"I was almost certain I'd told all of you." Judith

stuck the thimble on her finger. "Noah and Keturah were driving home from meeting and were caught in a flash flood. They both drowned." She frowned. "Fortunately, the *kinner* weren't feeling well and had stayed home with the oldest. It wonders me if sickness isn't a blessing sometimes."

"*Ach*, no, that's terrible! What happened to the *kinner*? Did they move to a relative's house?"

"I'm not sure. I'd heard that one of the older children was planning to get married." She tapped her chin. "Thomas, I think. Maybe he and his wife took the *kinner* in."

Lillianna's heart sank. *Thomas is married? That must be why he'd stopped writing. I wish he would have at least told me.* She felt a tear forming and abruptly stood up from her chair. "I—I need to go to the bathroom." Lillianna quickly rushed out of the room.

No. God, please don't let Thomas be married.

It seemed the older she became, the more aware of her age she was. Carolanne's sudden wedding had thrown her for a loop. Now that her best friend was married, they wouldn't have as much time together. Lillianna felt lost, and a little lonely, she admitted. If only there was a way she could see Thomas again, then she'd know for sure whether he was married or not. Carolanne had been a great friend since her family moved to Ohio, but their friendship never rivaled the close companionship she and Thomas had once shared.

Where are you, Tommy?

Chapter Two

Lillianna hastily gathered the laundry off the clothesline and glanced heavenward. The dreary clouds would be giving way any second now. A low rumble and warm droplets on her arms confirmed her prediction. She picked up the laundry basket and skittered to the house. The moment she stepped onto the porch, the clouds unleashed their fury.

"Mandy, come help your sister with the laundry," *Mamm* called from the kitchen.

Lillianna frowned. "I can manage." Her sister's idea of help was anything but.

"She needs the practice," *Mamm* insisted.

Mandy entered the kitchen and headed straight for the oven. "Mm…it smells *gut*, *Mamm*. What are you making?"

"Close that right now. You're going to let all the heat out," *Mamm* said. "I'm making supper. You were supposed to help, remember?"

"You know I don't like helping in the kitchen,"

Amanda protested. "And I don't like doing laundry, neither." She frowned at Lillianna. "Can't Lilly do it herself? She don't need me."

"Yes, you are going to help. You need to learn these things. You'll be doing them all yourself someday."

"I don't think I want to get married. It's too much work. I think I'm just gonna become *Englisch.* They're lucky, they get to do whatever they want."

"You best not let your father hear you talking like that. Now go help your sister before I send you out to the woodshed," *Mamm's* exasperated voice creaked.

"But *Mamm*—"

"Now!"

"Fine."

Lillianna shook her head. There's no way *she* would have gotten away with that kind of behavior. It seems her folks had become lackadaisical in their parenting with the last few *kinner.* "Let's take these up to my bedroom," she said to her twelve-year-old sister.

Amanda helped lay each item out on the bed without complaint. "I don't get you, Lilly."

"What do you mean, you don't 'get' me?" Lillianna raised her eyebrows.

"Well, you're nineteen, ain't so?"

Oh no, where is this conversation going? She nodded.

"Why are ya here? Why don't you go off and see what the *Englisch* world is like?"

Lillianna laughed. "Where would I go? I don't know anybody out there."

"You could go look for your beau."

"I don't have a beau." She took a dress and slipped it onto a hanger.

"How about Thomas?"

Lillianna could feel heat rising to her cheeks. *Nobody knew about me and Tommy.* "Thomas who?"

"You know. Thomas. The one you was kissin' at the creek a long time ago."

"Where did you hear that?"

"I seen you. I was hiding behind the tree." A sly grin crept over her face.

"You shouldn't have been. It's not right to spy on other people."

"But *Mamm* and *Dat* do. I sometimes see them creep to the top of the stairs to listen when Rosemary's beau comes over."

Lillianna gasped. "You should be sleeping at that hour. It's none of your business what *Mamm* and *Dat* do. They're parents. Parents do that kind of stuff."

"How come it's all right for them but not me?"

"Because it's their job to protect their children. Your job is to obey your folks, and right now that means helping me with this laundry instead of gazing out at the storm."

"I would go find Thomas if I were you." Mandy snatched up a pair of *Dat's* trousers.

Lillianna chuckled. "And how do you propose I do that?"

"Go to Pennsylvania and see if he's still there. If he's not, ask questions. I'm sure nosy ol' Ruth will give you some answers."

Lillianna gasped again. "Amanda Zook, you need to watch what you say about your elders. That's disrespectful."

"But it's true!"

"Maybe so, but we don't talk about it."

"Why not?" She frowned.

"Well, because. We're not supposed to speak evil of our neighbor, even if it is true."

"But she's not our neighbor. Ain't never been."

"Mandy, that's enough." She stared at the pile of clothes that still needed to be put away. "We need to get these done before *Mamm* calls us down for supper. Please stop talking and help me."

"Okay. But I'd still go see your beau."

"He's not my beau."

"Mm-hmm."

Lillianna had to bite her tongue. If not, they'd be here all evening.

The pounding rain prevented Lillianna from sleeping. She pulled her Nine Patch heart quilt up to her chin and smiled when a flash of lightning illuminated her entire bedroom. She'd always loved storms. Well, unless she was out driving in them.

She shivered when she thought of Thomas' folks drowning in that flash flood. Had it been a night like tonight when the heavens poured out water by the bucketful? She could only imagine what it must've been like for the *kinner*. *What would I have done if we'd lost* Mamm *and* Dat*?* With all her heart, she wished she could have been there for Tommy. Had someone else stepped in and provided the comfort she might have given? *If only Tommy had written.*

Lillianna thought back on her earlier conversation with Mandy. What *would* Thomas think if she just showed up on his doorstep out of the blue? Would he want to talk to her? What would his wife say about an old friend showing up to see her husband? *If* he was married, which she was still uncertain of. If she knew for a fact that he was married, she wouldn't even be contemplating the idea. She needed to find out. But if he wasn't married, what other reason was there for him to not write back?

A rumble of thunder in the distance informed Lillianna that the storm was moving on. Hopefully, she could get some sleep now. Otherwise, she'd be exhausted when she started her new job at the restaurant tomorrow.

"You know, Lillianna, Samuel is from Pennsylvania. It wonders me if he might know anyone from your old district," Carolanne commented.

Lillianna perked up. "I'd never thought of that."

"He said he lived near Paradise, in Bishop Hostettler's district. Is that close to where you're from?" Carolanne held the reins steady as a car passed them on the road. "Didn't you say something about Paradise before?"

"*Jah!* They were just a few miles away. Do you think he knows anyone from Bishop Mast's district?" Lillianna's stomach turned cartwheels at the possibility of learning Thomas' whereabouts. She needed to find out if he really had married. And who. For some reason, she couldn't picture Thomas with any of the *maed* from their old district.

"I could ask."

"That would be *wunderbaar*, Carolanne!" She squeezed her friend's arm briefly, unable to suppress her excitement. "I'm so glad you asked me to come shopping today."

"I needed more supplies for the bake shop, and I needed a break. It seems like it's been forever since we've spent time together."

"*Jah.* I'm glad I didn't have to go into the restaurant today, otherwise I wouldn't have been able to come. It seems like that job takes up so much of my time." Lillianna sighed.

"At least you're able to save up money to go to Pennsylvania."

"*Jah.* The job is a blessing." She surveyed Carolanne's content features. "So, how is married life?"

"It's different, for certain sure, but I'm enjoying it. Samuel is all I ever could have hoped for." Carolanne smiled.

"Really?" Lillianna raised her eyebrows.

"Why do you act so surprised?"

"You know I have my doubts about Samuel."

"I do."

"Aren't you the least bit concerned? Don't you want to know why he just moved here out of the blue? Didn't his coming seem a little suspicious? Mysterious? I don't know. I just know that if it was me, I'd have a lot of questions."

"Lilly, have you ever considered the possibility that some things are better left unsaid?" Carolanne offered her easy smile, reminding Lillianna how different they were.

"But what if he had a girlfriend in Pennsylvania? What if—"

"I'd rather not know. Look, Lillianna, he's my husband. If he wanted me to know about his past, he would've told me. Did he have a girlfriend while we were courting through letters? I don't know, and honestly, I don't care. I trust him. And he married *me*. If he loved someone else, why would he marry *me*?"

"You're probably right. I'm sorry. You know I let my imagination get the best of me sometimes," Lillianna conceded. "I can't help but worry about my best friend."

"I know."

"Samuel does seem like a nice guy," she admitted.

"He is. Really."

"So, is he a good kisser?"

Carolanne gasped. "I can't believe you're asking that!"

Lillianna laughed. "Never mind, you don't have to answer."

Chapter Three

"So, Lilly, *Dat* and *Mamm* have been talking about you a lot lately." Amanda boasted a satisfactory smile.

"Mm…hm." Lillianna knew better not to take her bait. She always spilled the beans anyhow, whether she intended to or not.

"*Mamm* said she was getting worried 'cause most young folks are baptized into the church by eighteen or so."

"Some join young and others don't ever join."

"You aren't thinkin' of not joinin' at all, are ya? Just because you don't have a beau doesn't mean ya can't get baptized. I heard of folks getting baptized at twenty-four and you ain't that old yet."

Lillianna shook her head. "What difference is a year? I don't have peace about joining yet."

"*Dat* said they were talking about you leaving."

"I have no plans to leave."

"What if they make you?"

Lilly shrugged. "If they make me, they make me. Maybe God has a different plan for my life."

"Well, I'm joinin' next time around. James said—" Amanda gasped and covered her mouth.

Lillianna laughed.

"Promise you won't tell *Mamm* or *Dat* anything about James," Mandy pleaded. "I don't think they care much for him."

"It's up to you to do the choosin' and the tellin'. Just make sure that you choose well, because you've got to live with your choice for the rest of your life," Lillianna advised.

"Do you think it's better to not marry anyone and become an *alt maedel* than to marry the wrong person?"

"I think so."

"Well, how do you know it's the right person?"

"I would pray about it and ask God to show me if it's the right person or not. If it's the right person, God will give you peace about it. But just make sure you're listening to God and not your own heart."

Amanda's head tilted. "I thought I was supposed to follow my heart."

"Following your heart will lead you into sin. Sin is what we naturally want to do. Our hearts crave it. The Bible says that the heart is deceitful and desperately wicked. We need to follow God's Word, not our hearts."

Lillianna thought on her own words. Was she following her heart in going to find Thomas or was she following God's will? *God, if you don't want me to go to Pennsylvania, please make it clear. I desire to do Your will.*

Lillianna smoothed out *Mamm's* dress over the ironing board and took one of the small irons off the woodstove. As she forced the wrinkles from the dress, she pondered her musings of late. Today was the day. It was time to speak with *Dat* and *Mamm* about her decision. For better or worse, her mind was made up.

She'd thought long and hard. God hadn't given her a definite yes on the matter, but she hadn't heard a no either. Everybody expected her to get baptized and join the church, so that's what she planned to do.

Who knows if she'd ever see Thomas again? She did still plan to go to Pennsylvania, but since Samuel hadn't found any good news, Lillianna figured searching for Tommy would most likely be a lost cause. When and if she learned of Tommy's whereabouts, she'd decide her next course of action. But for now, to make the bishop happy and set *Dat's* and *Mamm's* minds at ease, she would consent to be baptized.

She prayed she was making the right decision.

Chapter Four

Lillianna took the handkerchief from her apron pocket and wiped the perspiration from her brow. She glanced up at the clock on the wall and grinned. Just thirty more minutes and her shift would be over.

Working at the restaurant had been enjoyable and she'd had the opportunity to meet all sorts of people. Just last week, a congressman stopped in and left her a nice tip. The man was friendly, and good-looking, she admitted. But it seemed no man could hold a candle to Thomas. Until she knew without a doubt that he was married, she would hold out hope.

Samuel had once again enquired about Thomas on her behalf, but no one knew for certain of his whereabouts. He reminded her that the information he'd gotten could be wrong, since it had come from a neighboring district and not from Thomas' district directly.

So, Lillianna had made up her mind. She would go back to her old Amish district in Pennsylvania and find her own answers. For better or worse, she had to know the truth. Never did she think it would be *five years* before she'd saved up enough money to go. Nor did she think she'd be twenty-four and still single. She made a decent amount of money working at the restaurant, but the majority had to go to her folks, which she did not begrudge because that was their way. As a consequence, she was only allowed to keep a small portion of her earnings.

In just a few more months, her anticipated trip would be fully-funded. As the day grew closer, she could barely contain her excitement or her anxiety. Carolanne reminded her many times that whatever she discovered in Pennsylvania would be God's will. She just hoped that she'd be able to handle it.

Carolanne had Lillianna worried. She'd been sick a lot lately. So ill, in fact, that she'd taken an extended vacation from the bakery. Samuel was near certain what Carolanne's condition was: she was expecting a *boppli*. They hadn't visited the doctor yet to confirm it, but they planned on going today. As soon as her shift at the restaurant ended, she would stop by the Beachys' to hear the confirmation.

Lillianna entered Carolanne and Samuel's home. An ominous feeling pricked her soul. Something wasn't right. Samuel's greeting wasn't anything like his normal demeanor. Lillianna had expected Carolanne's husband to be thrilled beyond belief, but that wasn't the impression she'd gotten. She recognized something in his eyes. Was it fear? Uncertainty?

"*Ach*, Lillianna! I'm so happy to see you. Would you like some tea?" Carolanne offered.

"*Jah*. Tea would be nice, *denki*." Lillianna studied her friend. Carolanne appeared normal. She didn't portray a bit of the insecurity she'd noticed in Samuel's countenance. Perhaps she was overreacting.

"How have things been at the restaurant?"

"*Gut*. How did your doctor appointment go?"

"Well," Carolanne smiled, "I'm not expecting a *boppli*."

Lillianna nodded, urging her to continue.

"Looks like I'll get to go to Heaven soon."

"What?" Lillianna frowned. "What's going on, Carolanne?" Goose bumps rose on her arms.

"Lilly, I have cancer."

Lillianna's jaw dropped. "But you're so young."

Carolanne rushed on. "Cancer happens to young and old. The doctors say it's too far gone to do anything about it." Tears surfaced in Carolanne's eyes, but she continued to smile. "I'm not scared. I just hope that Samuel…"

"Samuel?"

"Well, do you think maybe you might marry him when I'm gone?"

Lillianna was at a loss for words.

"I mean, you don't have to. I'm just worried about him is all. And since you're not hitched yet, I thought—"

"I don't know, Carolanne. That might not be God's will." How could she even think about marrying her best friend's husband? Especially when Carolanne was still alive.

"If you'd just consider it… You would like him, I promise. He is kind. He's been very *gut* to me." She wiped a tear away. "If you don't find your Thomas, or discover that he's married?"

"I can't make any promises, Carolanne, but I will think on it." She hesitated. "But not until after you've gone, which I hope isn't for a long, long time."

"*Denki*, Lilly. You are a *gut* friend."

Chapter Five

"Lilly, there is a group of Amish young folks going to the Grand Canyon next week," Carolanne reminded Lillianna.

"*Jah*, I know. It sounds like a lot of fun."

"The bishop asked if Samuel and I would like to go along to chaperone. Since we aren't going to California until next month, Samuel wants to go."

Lilly smiled. The Grand Canyon sounded like an exciting place to visit, but she intended to use her extra money to look for Thomas.

"I want you to go too." Carolanne's eyes reflected the desire in her words.

Lillianna frowned. How could she say no to her dying best friend? "How much will it cost?"

"Samuel insists on paying for you. We know that you've been saving up to go to Pennsylvania."

"Can he afford it? I know how he's been talking about takin' you to California." Tears came to her eyes as she thought about losing Carolanne.

"Samuel is a *gut* saver and his buggy shop has done very well. We will have plenty," Carolanne assured. "And there will be plenty when I'm gone." She patted Lilly's hand.

"Don't talk like that, please. I don't want to think about you not being here." She wiped a tear.

Carolanne shrugged. "We all have to go sometime. I'm not afraid; I have Jesus. God will take my hand and I'll step into Heaven."

"I wish I was as sure as you are."

"You can be, you know. Just ask Jesus to save you and He will."

"I don't know. My family never really believed all that. Bishop Mast's district had a different *Ordnung*."

"What did Bishop Mast teach?"

Lillianna shrugged. "Same as most, I guess. It's prideful to say you're saved. Only God can know it for sure. We just do our best and hope we're good enough to get to Heaven."

"If that's the case, then I'm sad to say that none of Bishop Mast's followers are going to make it to Heaven."

Lillianna gasped. How could Carolanne say such things? *I am a good Amish woman.*

"If you and the others in your former district are not trusting in Christ to save you, then you have *no* hope of Heaven at all. God clearly says that Jesus is the only way to Heaven. No church rules can change what God has said in His Word. If you're trusting in anything else—your works, being Amish, your folks, whatever—you *will* go to Hell."

Lillianna could feel the blood rushing to her cheeks. She dearly loved Carolanne, but her words were bothersome. "But I've never done anything really bad. I've never killed anyone and I've always tried to be kind to others. I don't understand. Why would God make me go to Hell for being a good person?"

"People aren't barred from Heaven because they're bad people. Lilly, have you ever told a lie?"

"Yes."

"What does that make you?"

"A liar. So what? Everyone has lied. Nobody's perfect, not even you."

"Which is why we *all* need Jesus. I need Him just as much as you do. Don't you see, Lilly? We are sinners. When we bring what we think are our good works to God, He sees them as filthy, dirty rags. They are an insult to Him. He is absolute holiness, absolute perfectness. Anything less than perfection is not acceptable in His presence."

Lillianna frowned.

"But He loved mankind, so He sent His Son, Jesus Christ, to die to pay our sin debt. He was the only acceptable sacrifice because He was without sin, perfect in every way. It is only by His blood that our sins can be washed away."

She rubbed her temples. "I don't understand."

Carolanne continued on. "When we accept

Christ's payment for our sin, we are acknowledging that we cannot make it to Heaven on our own. You are saying to God that you repent of your unbelief and now believe according to the Truth of God's Word. When you trust Jesus, you receive *His* righteousness so that when you stand before God, He sees complete and total perfection. He sees Christ, your substitute. He is the only way to get rid of your sins. No *Ordnung* or religion could ever do that. No good deeds could ever do that. Only the blood of Jesus."

"But how can I do that? And how can I know for sure that is the way to Heaven?"

"You can know because that is what God says in His Word. God does not lie." Carolanne touched Lilly's shoulder. "He says, 'That if thou shalt confess with thy mouth the Lord Jesus, and shalt believe in thine heart that God hath raised him from the dead, thou shalt be saved. For with the heart man believeth unto righteousness; and with the mouth confession is made unto salvation… For whosoever shall call upon the name of the Lord shall be saved.'" Carolanne's expression exuded hope. "Do you want Jesus to save you, Lilly?"

Tears pricked her eyes. "*Jah*, I do."

Chapter Six

The slow ticking of the clock on the wall nearly drove Lillianna crazy. How long did it take to say, "Okay, Lillianna, your name has been considered for membership"? Were the leaders deliberately stalling to make her nervous?

The group of ministers was presently congregated near a corner in the house. One of the ministers glanced her way, then turned back and spoke with the others once again. She couldn't help feeling like the odd one out.

Finally, the men turned to her. "We have some concerns," one of the ministers admitted.

Oh great. They're not going to let me go on the trip. How she hated the thought of staying back while her moments with Carolanne were precious.

"Frankly, we're questioning your sincerity in this matter."

"What?"

"You've made no indication nor shown any desire to be baptized until now. Are you not joining the church in order to be eligible to marry a certain soon-to-be widower?" the deacon asked.

Lillianna's jaw dropped. She was speechless.

"This is a serious matter."

"Wha—? No! That is *not* why I'm getting baptized." She could scarcely believe these men would mention anything of the sort. Where did they hear of such things? Was that the latest talk in their community? That she was just waiting for Carolanne to die so she could snatch Samuel? The thought sickened her.

"What are your reasons, then?"

She felt like pulling her hair out. Was this really such a difficult thing? "I want to join the church, become a voting member, agree to live by the same rules that the other members live by."

The men looked at one another and nodded in satisfaction. "Very well. The classes will begin in two weeks."

Lillianna breathed a sigh of relief. They hadn't mentioned anything about not going on the trip. Now, she could pack for the trip without fear of missing her membership classes.

Lillianna wanted to be excited about this trip— really, she did. But the fact that she was sitting next to Carolanne, and this would most likely be one of the last times they spent together, greatly dampened her spirit. She couldn't suppress the foreboding aura that lingered in her mind.

She glanced over at Samuel, who sat on the bench seat just over on the other side of Carolanne, next to the van door. What must he be thinking? How could one mentally prepare himself for the death of a loved one? She'd heard that the death of a spouse was one of the most difficult life events to ever happen. Yet, death was a natural thing; no one escapes it.

Carolanne, on the other hand, appeared bright and cheerful. With each mile, it seemed she pointed out another feature of God's wonderful creation. It was like watching a child dip his hand into a jar of rock candy. Each color had its own flavor and she wanted to try every single one, or at least talk about it.

"Look! We just passed into Arizona. We should be there soon." Carolanne's eyes smiled.

"It'll still be several hours," the driver informed them.

"Oh, those rocks are so beautiful!"

Lillianna glanced at Samuel, and he, in turn, smiled at his wife. "She never ceases to find beauty in the ordinary. Just look at me." He chuckled.

"Samuel Beachy, you are anything but ordinary," Carolanne insisted. "You are the sweetest, most handsome man that God ever made."

Lillianna smiled. Carolanne was right in choosing Samuel for a mate; they were perfect for each other. She wondered if there was anyone out there that completed *her*.

Thomas. The name seemed to come as a whisper on the wind. It was so real, she momentarily glanced around to see if anyone else had heard it. Nobody had.

It was only a matter of time before she made her way to Pennsylvania. The thought made butterflies flitter in her stomach.

"If those people over there keep staring at us, I'm going to walk over and tell them to quit being so rude," Marcus complained.

"You'll do no such thing, Marcus," Samuel warned, pointing two fingers in Marcus' direction.

Lillianna was thankful that Samuel was made the person in charge on this trip.

"They've probably never seen any Amish before. I don't think there are many who come out this way," Carolanne added.

"There are some in Colorado, and I heard a new settlement started up in Idaho as well," Samuel said.

"Really? I didn't know that some came way out west." Lillianna's brow rose.

"They're still staring." Marcus glared.

"Well, aren't *you* staring at them too?" Another girl from their group laughed.

"Let's go have a gander at another area. Who's got the camera?" Samuel asked.

"I do." Lillianna held it up. She walked behind the group and discreetly took pictures of Carolanne and Samuel. She wanted to have something to remember her friend by after she was gone, even if it was *verboten*.

"Uh oh." She glanced up and found Marcus at her side. "Better delete that one."

"Please mind your own business, Marcus. I'm taking whatever pictures I want to. It's *my* camera." Lillianna frowned.

"Relax, Lilly. I was joking."

"You'd better be."

"Come on, let's catch up with the others before we lose them."

"Ach, this wind is crazy!" Lillianna said as another strand of hair fell loose from her bun. She spied a restroom sign that pointed to facilities around the corner. "I need to use the bathroom. Do you need to go?"

Carolanne shook her head, so Lillianna headed in that direction. "I shouldn't be long," she called back over her shoulder.

Lillianna stepped out from the stall and quickly washed and dried her hands. She smoothed the sides of her hair with a little water from the faucet and tucked the disobedient strands behind her ears. She grimaced when she looked into the mirror. What she really needed was to redo the whole mess, but it would take much longer than her allotted time. This would have to do until she arrived at the motel. She adjusted her *kapp*, then stepped out of the restroom to go meet up with the rest of the group.

A sudden obstacle sent Lillianna's bottom straight to the concrete ground.

"Oh, I'm so sorry, miss!" a deep voice apologized.

The grip on her arm forced her to look up into the face concealed by a thin goatee and sunglasses. It was one of the curious men she'd seen before. Lillianna's cheeks flushed. "*Ach*, I should have been looking where I was going."

The man moved his sunglasses to the top of his head. "No, it's my faul—" His words stopped in mid-sentence; his mouth dropped open. The man's eyebrows shot up. "Lil? Lillianna Zook? Is it you?"

Chapter Seven

Lillianna's heart quickened. There's only *one* person who had ever called her "Lil". She looked closer. *Could it be?*

"I'm Tommy! Thomas Girod. Do you remember me?"

Do I ever! She finally found her voice. "*Jah*. I remember."

Perhaps Thomas couldn't help it, but he pulled her into his arms and kissed her cheek lightly. "It's so good to see you!"

Apparently, he isn't married! Lillianna pulled away and looked to see if anyone from the group had noticed her in the embrace of an *Englischer*. She'd get an earful from the leaders, to be sure, if word ever got back.

"Oh, no. Uh, your husband isn't around, is he?" Thomas' clumsy words tumbled out. "I'm sorry. I didn't even consider that you might be married. What was I thinking?" Worry creased his brow.

Lillianna laughed. "No, I'm not married. I just… you just took me by surprise is all. I can hardly believe it's you."

His eyes swept over her once again. "Wow, you look great! I can't believe this! What on earth are you doing here?"

"Visiting the Grand Canyon," she teased.

Thomas chuckled. "Really? I wouldn't have guessed."

"A group of us are here from Ohio," she clarified. "And you?"

He shrugged. "It's just me and my friend Tyrone. I think he's waiting for me over in the museum. Would you like to come meet him?"

"Uh, sure. Let me check with the group first."

Thomas walked beside her and quickly spotted the group of young Amish people. He glanced down at his shorts and T-shirt and briefly wished he'd worn long pants. Oh well, he wasn't Amish anymore, and didn't plan to ever be again.

"Thomas, this is my friend Carolanne and her husband, Samuel," Lillianna said.

Thomas offered his hand to Samuel and nodded politely to Carolanne. "Nice to meet you. You don't mind if I steal Lil for a little bit, do you?"

"Lil, huh?" Carolanne echoed.

Lillianna smiled, sending her friend a look of warning. "Tommy is from my former Amish community in Pennsylvania."

"Sorry, but the group is supposed to stay together," Marcus stepped forward.

Lillianna frowned at him.

"I'm not opposed to Lillianna going with you, if she wants to," Samuel said. He turned to Lillianna. "Make sure you're not back too late."

Lillianna nodded.

"Don't forget supper at six," Marcus butted in.

Thomas frowned and glanced at Lillianna. "Oh, I'd hoped to have supper with you, but if—"

"She'd love to have supper with you. You have a lot of catching up to do, *jah*?" Carolanne insisted.

Lillianna turned to Carolanne, communicating her gratitude. "I'll meet you back at the motel tonight. That is, if Thomas can give me a ride."

Thomas smiled. "You bet."

"Take your time." Carolanne gave her a knowing smile.

"You're great, you know that?" Lillianna winked.

"Shall we?" Thomas held out his elbow and Lillianna lightly clutched it. He led the way toward the museum and a few moments later, Lillianna spotted an African-American man waiting on a bench. "There he is."

"Who ya got there, brother?" The friendly man offered Lillianna a bright smile.

"This is Lil. Lillianna. We've known each other since we were knee-high to a grasshopper. She was one of my best friends. I haven't seen her in years."

"Well, I'm pleased to meet you, Lillianna," Tyrone said.

"*Denki.* Thank you. Nice to meet you too."

Thomas rubbed his forehead. "Hey, Ty. You don't mind if I skip out on you, do ya?"

"You gonna leave me high and dry?" Tyrone protested.

Lillianna felt bad that she interrupted their plans. "Oh no, we could—"

Thomas laughed. "He's jokin', Lil."

She studied Tyrone. He waved his hand in front of his face and chuckled. "You two go and have yourselves a great time."

Lillianna released an anxious breath and smiled. "Thank you, Tyrone."

"My friends call me 'Ty'."

She smiled. "Thanks, Ty."

"By the way, you might want to watch out for this guy. He'll get you into heaps of trouble," Tyrone warned.

Lillianna looked at Thomas and raised her brow. "Really? Hmm…so are you saying I shouldn't go with him?" She smiled.

"Nah, not really. Just wanted to give you a heads-up is all."

Thomas winked at Lillianna.

"I'll have to keep that in mind. Thanks for the warning, Ty."

Thomas navigated their way toward another area of the canyon.

"He's seems like a nice man." Lillianna hoped the breeze wouldn't pull her *kapp* off.

"Ty's been a good friend."

Lillianna stood at the guardrail overlooking a huge section of the canyon. She gasped as she beheld the magnificent natural wonder. Colorful bands accented the layers of reddish-brown, hard compacted rock that stretched for miles. Extraordinary deep valleys, sharp peaks that appeared as monuments and many plateaus defined the landscape. Several lone trees seemed to grow right out of the rock layers and she marveled at how they survived in the dry desert climate. Below, a tiny cerulean-blue river meandered through the bottom of the canyon. "Oh, my goodness! This is so beautiful."

"Pretty spectacular, huh? Nature is cool."

"God is a wonderful *gut* Creator, *jah*?"

"God has nothing to do with this, Lil." He grasped her hand and pulled her to a nearby sign. "See, the Colorado River formed this over millions of years. Look at all the layers in the rocks. It just proves the truth of evolution."

"Evolution?"

"Yes, evolution. You know, Lillianna, how the scientists say that we originated from primates millions of years ago."

"Primates?"

"Apes, monkeys, etcetera."

"You really believe that?"

"Of course. Most reputable scientists believe and

teach that. Wait. Don't tell me you *still* believe all that stuff about Adam and Eve and the Garden of Eden."

"*Jah*, I do."

Thomas chuckled. "You've got to be kidding me. Why do you still believe those fairy tales?"

"They're not fairy tales." Lillianna frowned.

"Why do you believe, Lil?"

Lillianna was speechless. She hadn't taken any classes on the origin of life, she just simply believed in what the Bible said.

"Look, you don't have an answer. You don't even know *why* you believe, Lil! Are you going to continue to live off your folks' faith your whole life? There's more out there that you've never even heard about, never even considered. Have you ever thought, even for just one second, that what you were taught was wrong? That it was all a lie? God is nothing more than a myth, Lillianna. It's just a concept that people made up to give themselves a sense of comfort."

Lillianna's mouth dropped open. Was this really Tommy? The boy she'd grown up with?

"Surprised? This is what happens when you actually start thinking for yourself. Education is a wonderful thing, Lil. It opens your mind and allows you to explore new possibilities. The reason you believe like you do is because it's all you've ever known. You were never taught to question." A bitter laugh escaped his lips. "We were never allowed to question *anything*. We didn't have a choice but to believe everything that was shoved down our throats."

"Is that what you think, Tommy?"

"Yes, it is."

"So, everyone who hasn't been to college like you is basically an idiot who can't think for themselves?"

"Whoa, whoa, whoa… I'm not calling you an idiot, if that's what you're thinking. I'm just trying to challenge you to think outside the box," Thomas asserted.

"So, if I 'think outside the box', which to you apparently means abandoning my faith in God, I'm not an idiot?"

He sighed. "Okay, let me backpedal here. I'm sorry, Lil. I didn't mean to offend you. Let's drop the subject."

"For now," she conceded.

"Man, what was I thinking bringing up a subject like that when we haven't seen each other in eons?"

"Subject dropped," she reminded him.

"Okay, so, dinner then?"

"*Jah*. That sounds *gut*."

"*Zehr gut*." He laughed as his stomach rumbled loudly.

Tommy doesn't believe in God? The thought troubled Lillianna to no end.

Chapter Eight

Thomas nodded to the waitress when she picked up their empty dinner plates. His gaze landed on the wonderful woman across the table. He drank in her presence—her delicate floral perfume, her silky flaxen hair, her pale blue eyes, her soft pink lips— the ones he'd had the pleasure of feeling against his. Once. Meeting Lillianna was the best gift anyone could have given him and he momentarily wondered if maybe there was a God after all. "I can't tell you how great it is to see you again, Lil."

Lillianna's beautiful grin captured his heart once again. She reminded him of all that was good and lovely, and caused him to temporarily ignore his current dire circumstances.

"Why did you stop writing to me?" Lil asked.

It was a simple question, but the answer was complicated. How could he tell her the truth of his past… or his present? He sucked in a breath. "You heard that my folks died?"

She nodded.

"It was a very dark time for me." Just talking about it conjured up images he'd rather forget—like his younger siblings begging him to stay. But he knew he couldn't. "I had to leave. I couldn't stay in that house with constant memories of *Dat* and *Mamm*."

"So that's when you became *Englisch*?"

He nodded and reached for her hand.

"I wish I could have been there to help you through that time."

"Me too." He rubbed the top of her hand with his thumb.

"I didn't even hear about it until a few years after it happened. My folks knew but nobody told me. If I'd known...well I don't know what I would have done. But I could have at least prayed for you."

"You're such a sweetheart, Lil." The waitress put the guest check upside down on their table. Thomas glanced around and noticed they were some of the last few patrons in the restaurant. "It looks like they're closing. We should probably go."

Thomas removed the motel key card from his wallet and inserted it into the slot in the door. When the green light showed, he opened the door and motioned Lillianna inside.

She frowned. "I'd better not."

"Please, Lil? I'm not ready for you to go yet. We haven't seen each other in so long and you'll be leaving soon. We've hardly had time to catch up. The lobby is closed. There is no other place to go," he reasoned. "Come in?"

"Maybe for just a little bit." She walked into his motel room, and a slight shiver tingled on her arms.

"Good. 'Cause if you wouldn't, I might've just had to set up chairs in the corridor." He chuckled.

"We could do that."

He shook his head. "I don't think so. Besides, there's something I've been wanting to discuss with you and it's not really something I'd like to tell the world."

What would he want to discuss in private? Maybe...no, she wouldn't get her hopes up. It was too soon.

Thomas offered her a chair at the small table in his room, and then walked over to the small coffee maker. "Want some coffee?"

"Sure." Anticipation quickened her heartbeat.

In short order, he brought two steaming mugs to the table along with cream and sugar. Thomas took the seat across from Lillianna. They sat quietly for a couple of minutes until Thomas gathered the nerve to speak his mind.

"There's really no way to sugarcoat what I have to say, Lil, so I'll just spill it." He sipped his coffee, then reached across the table and took her hand. His eyes met hers. "I'm dying."

Lillianna's heart pounded in her ears and her vision clouded as she realized what Tommy had said. This couldn't be right. "What?"

"I have terminal cancer. I don't have long to live."

God, no! Tears welled in Lillianna's eyes. She shook her head. "No. Not you too! Please, Thomas. Tell me you're teasing me."

"I wish I was."

"But we just met again. I… I can't lose you now."

"I'm sorry, Lil. Truly sorry."

"But you're going through treatment, aren't you? They can make you better, *jah*?" She didn't bother to brush her tears away.

"I did. My body didn't respond well to the chemo. It seemed like my cancer actually spread after going through the treatments. The oncologist said I'd probably be better off not continuing. Beside the fact that the treatments didn't work, they were also expensive."

"But you look fine—"

"I know. I didn't before, trust me. I'd lost all my hair, I was sicker than a dog, my strength was gone, I'd wished I was dead. But sometimes when chemo is stopped, patients will go into a brief remission. But the cancer always returns. That's part of the reason I'm here—enjoying the last of my days."

"I have some money. Not much, but it can help some."

"No, Lil. I appreciate it, though."

"So, that's it? You're just going to give up?"

"What else can I do?"

"Have you considered natural treatments? When I found out about Carolanne's cancer, I did some research on my own. Carolanne didn't want me to, but I did anyhow. I couldn't just let my best friend die. I found some clinics that have really good survival numbers, much better than treatment with chemotherapy. They treat cancer naturally with herbs and supplements and enemas—"

"Enemas?" He raised his eyebrows and a disgusted look flashed across his features.

"If it helps your body heal, why not?" She looked into his eyes. "This is your life, Tommy. You don't get another one. Please?"

"I thought you believed in God and all that eternal life stuff."

"My faith in God will only get *me* to Heaven. You need to have your own."

Thomas quickly changed the subject. "I guess if I could go through chemo, I can get through anything. How much do natural treatments cost?"

She sucked in a breath. "They're not cheap, although I know they're not as much as chemotherapy. I'll help you get the money."

Thomas frowned.

Lillianna stood at his side and grasped his hands. "*Please*, Tommy. I just found you. I don't want to lose you again. I can't lose you."

"I'll do anything for you, Lil. You know I will." Thomas stood up and tugged her hands, pulling her into his arms. While he held her close, it seemed as though time stood still. He bent down and pressed his lips to her neck, eventually making his way to her lips. "I love you."

"I love you too." Lillianna's heart hammered in her chest as she returned his impassioned kisses. Kissing Tommy was even more exhilarating than she'd dreamed. And wasn't this what she'd dreamed of—finding Tommy and spending the rest of her life with him? But how long would that be? She wouldn't dwell on that now. Couldn't.

Thomas took two steps backward and gently pulled her onto the bed. His hands caressed her back and neck and he moved closer to remove the space between them. "Lil? Let's…"

What am I doing? Lillianna forced herself away. She couldn't allow herself to get caught up in the moment. "This is a bad idea, Tommy."

He gently pulled her close again and stroked her hair. "No, this is a very *good* idea," he murmured, his lips meeting her neckline.

"I need to go." She forced herself to break contact.

"Please, Lil?" His eyes begged.

"But, it's not right." Lillianna found controlling her heartbeat difficult as her desire toward Tommy increased at an uncomfortable speed. With all her heart, she wanted to stay. She wanted to revel in the caress of his lips against hers. She wanted to let Tommy hold her forever.

"It feels right to me."

God, help me. "I can't, Tommy."

"But, Lil, we might never get this chance again. I mean, if I die…" He hung his head.

His manipulation tactic felt like a slap in the face. "So, you only want me because you're dying? Is that what you're saying, Tommy? Is that why you're showing me affection?"

"No. Of course not! I want you because I love you."

"Because you love me… What exactly does that mean?"

"Why are you making this so complicated?" His hands clenched at his sides. "I love you. You love me. What else matters, Lil?" His tone gentled and he softly moved a wisp of hair that had fallen on her neck where his lips had been a moment ago.

"A lot matters. We aren't married, Thomas. It wouldn't be right. Love is supposed to be patient." She frowned. "Besides, I'm Amish and you are not."

He shook his head, his countenance fraught with…*repulsion*? "You've been baptized?"

"I'm taking classes soon."

Thomas grasped Lillianna's hands with urgency. "Please don't join yet. Will you do that for me? Wait till I die, until there's no chance of us being together. If I can somehow beat this cancer, if there's a chance, I want to marry you."

Lillianna's heart stopped. Wasn't this what she'd been dreaming of her entire life? Tommy returning to marry her and the two of them creating a big, beautiful family together, then living out the rest of their days on the farm enjoying sunrises and sunsets as they sat on their wraparound porch holding hands?

But this—*this*—was different. Her dream hadn't included an incurable disease. It didn't include Tommy dying young and leaving her alone all her days, like Samuel was certain to be. And her dream certainly didn't include an eternity without Tommy by her side. Could she convince Tommy that he *needed* God? Would Thomas expect her to leave the Amish or would he eventually agree to join the church too?

Amid her confusing thoughts, she pondered Tommy's words. She caught the sadness in his eyes. And the hopefulness. He waited patiently for her reply.

She didn't have all the answers now, but there was one thing she did know. She wasn't about to lose Tommy again. "I'll wait for you."

Thomas released a drawn-out breath, then pulled her close. "Thanks, Lil. You don't know how much this means to me."

Lillianna glanced at the digital alarm clock on the nightstand. "It's getting late. I better go. I don't want the others to worry about me."

"I wish you could stay all night. We could—" His lips brushed her cheek.

"*Thomas*…" she warned.

"I know. Okay." He gallantly opened the door. "May I walk you home?"

She giggled. "I'm just ten doors down."

"All right, then just a goodnight kiss." He bent down and lingered at her lips. "Mm… I'm going to have sweet dreams tonight."

Lillianna reluctantly broke away, realizing they were halfway in the hallway and someone might see them. "Good night, Tommy."

Chapter Nine

Lillianna could barely stay focused on her wait-ressing duties. She'd been counting the days until Tommy's arrival and today was the day. Instead of asking for the day off, like a *dummkopp*, she'd agreed to work. That had been a mistake. Hopefully her em-ployer would overlook all the blunders she'd been making. She'd be surprised if he still wanted her to return next week after Thomas left.

To her astonishment, her folks agreed to let Tommy stay in their *dawdi haus* while he was visit-ing. Of course, she'd left out one little detail about Tommy. They didn't know he was *Englisch*. She was somewhat nervous about him coming and her folks' reaction, but she knew they probably would have said no if they'd known. Lillianna was certain the rea-son they'd said yes in the first place was in hopes of her finding a beau. She had found one all right, but they most likely weren't going to be thrilled about his spiritual state.

But that was okay. She was certain that as soon as they heard about Tommy's health predicament, they'd be sympathetic toward his plight. Lillianna had a plan, hopefully one that would earn Thomas enough money to go through natural treatments.

"Why don't you go ahead and take off the rest of the day?"

Lillianna jumped at her employer's words and she dropped the silverware in her hands. Pink tinged her cheeks when she realized she'd been daydreaming again. She hastily picked up the silverware. "I'm sorry."

"No need to apologize. I can tell you have a lot on your mind. Just come back next week with a clear head, okay?"

She dipped her head. "*Denki.*"

"And don't forget to pick up your check in the back office," he reminded.

There was no way Lillianna was going to forget her check. That was mostly the reason she'd decided to come in today. She would use her portion of that money and everything she'd been saving up for the trip to Pennsylvania, which was now unnecessary, for Thomas' treatments. She only hoped they could raise the remainder of the needed money quickly. Time was not on their side.

"Lilly, you'll never guess who's here." Mandy's singsong voice giggled.

Lillianna's eyes widened. "Tommy's here already?

Oh no, I'd hoped to have time to take a shower." She bit her bottom lip. "Where is he?"

"*Mamm's* showing him to the *dawdi haus*. She and *Dat* didn't look too happy." Amanda raised her eyebrows. "They didn't know he was an *Englischer*."

"I know."

"Is he in the *Bann*?"

"I don't know. I didn't ask him." Lillianna hadn't even thought that Tommy might be shunned. "It doesn't matter. He needs our help."

"I think *Mamm* and *Dat* want to talk to you." Mandy frowned.

"*Jah*, I'd 'spect so." Lillianna sighed. *Might as well get it over with.*

Lillianna reached up into the cupboard to retrieve the plates they'd be using for supper this evening. She still hadn't seen Thomas or her folks, but figured they'd confront her soon enough.

She gasped when she felt strong arms encircle her waist. Apparently Tommy had found his way into the kitchen. She turned into his embrace and allowed a brief kiss. It wouldn't do for her folks to come in and find them being intimate. That wasn't their way. Private things were best kept private.

"Hey, beautiful." Tommy's eyes sparkled. She could look into those eyes forever.

"I'm so glad you made it." She grimaced. "Did my folks give you a hard time?"

"Nah, they were pretty cool. They did look a little surprised, though."

"I didn't tell them you're *Englisch* now."

He chuckled. "I figured it must've been something like that. I told them that I'd never been shunned, so I think that might have smoothed things over a bit."

"What did they say?"

"They asked if I had plans to join the church."

Lillianna's eyes widened. "What did you tell them?"

"I said I didn't think I had time to join the church. I think they understood."

"Would you ever consider it?"

"Becoming Amish?" He frowned. "Lil, you know my thoughts on that."

"I know, but I was hoping—"

"Let's just take one day at a time, okay? Who knows what the future holds?"

God does. But she wouldn't speak those words aloud. She wanted her time with Tommy to be pleasant, not filled with arguments and disagreements. What *would* they do about their future—if they had one?

An unquenchable thirst drove Lillianna downstairs for a glass of water. The household was asleep now, but she couldn't seem to find the rest she needed. There were so many things on her mind— Carolanne and Samuel, who were in California at present, Tommy's illness and the lack of money for his treatments, and her relationship with Thomas.

How would they ever be able to work out their differences? She had no clue. Could an atheist and a Christian really dwell together in unity? She didn't think so.

"Couldn't sleep either?"

She turned at the sound of her mother's voice. "*Mamm*. No, I've been thinking a lot."

"About Thomas?"

"*Jah*, mostly." Her chest heaved. "I just found him and I don't want to let him go." She wiped a tear away.

"Loving someone can be hard at times. You risk a lot when you love—your heart and soul, at the least. Love is the most important and most rewarding investment you can make in another person." Her mother sat across the table and sipped water from her glass.

"You don't mind that Thomas is not Amish?"

"We all have to choose our own way, Lilly. God lays out a path for each of us; it is up to us whether we will walk in it or not."

"But how do we know if it is the right one?"

"If it is God's will, it will align with His Word. If it does not, then we know it is not His will. God will never lead us to do something against His Word."

Lillianna's lip trembled. "Tommy says he doesn't believe in God."

"That's too bad. At least God believes in him, *jah*?

And He says that a little faith can move mountains, *ain't so*?" Her mother briefly touched her forearm.

"*Jah*."

"Let's pray for Thomas and perhaps *Der Herr* will open his eyes to the truth."

"*Denki, Mamm*."

Chapter Ten

Lillianna took out the list she'd written down on notebook paper and looked at the others who sat around the table. "Okay, so here's the list of things we need to do this week: find donations for the auction—"

"Wait a minute." Thomas' eyebrows narrowed. "You want to have an auction? Don't those things take months, or at least weeks, to plan? I don't see how we're going to have enough time."

Lillianna nodded. "We'll do an online auction. You can do one or three days, however long or short you want to. I have an *Englisch* friend at work who does it all the time. She already said she'd help any way she can."

He snapped his fingers. "You're amazing."

"I think I might know someone who might donate a quilt," Amanda said.

"That's perfect. We need big items that will bring in a lot of money." Lillianna grinned. "Now back to my list. Do you think anyone would be willing to do-nate cash?" She directed the question at her mother.

"I'm not sure. You can ask Deacon Miller to make an announcement at meeting, but since Thomas isn't Amish..." She shrugged. "We can try."

Lillianna cast an apologetic smile at Tommy. "On Thursday and Friday is the yard sale, and on Satur-day we'll have the car wash. Mandy, you said you have volunteers for that, right?"

Amanda nodded.

"Great. So I think we're all set." Lillianna tapped her chin. "What do you think of an ice cream social on Tuesday night?"

Her mother smiled. "Who's going to make the ice cream?"

"I was hoping you and *Dat* would? Please?"

"I'll talk to your father."

Thomas weaved his fingers together and cracked his knuckles. "Wow. This is going to be one busy week."

"It'll be worth it." Lillianna's smile exuded con-fidence.

"I hope you're right."

"Me too. I'm not losing you without a fight."

"Nor I, you."

The day was nearly over. In the last week, they'd raised exactly $2,327. Although she was thankful for those who gave, she felt like crumbling to the ground and having a good cry.

She'd failed Tommy. This was only a portion of the monies needed for his treatments. Perhaps she could get a loan of some sort.

Lillianna picked up a bucket of soapy water. "Okay, let's go ahead and start cleaning up," her resigned voice trembled.

"It's okay, Lil. You did your best." Tommy's arm draped over her shoulders.

She swiped at a tear. "I wanted to do more. Tommy, you need those treatments."

"Excuse me." A man in a fancy sports car pulled up to the gas station. "Is the car wash still open?"

Lillianna looked at Tommy and he nodded. "*Jah*, it's open."

"Just pull your car up to the side of the building and make sure all the windows are closed," Thomas informed the man. He turned to the other volunteers. "Okay, guys, we got one more."

The others waited for the man to exit his vehicle and then started hosing the car down with water.

The man walked over to Lillianna. "You look awfully familiar. Do I know you from somewhere?"

She shook her head. "I don't think so."

"Wait a minute. You work at the restaurant downtown, don't you?"

"*Jah*."

Thomas came near to be sure this man wasn't hitting on his girl.

The man laughed. "I guess I didn't leave a big enough tip if you don't remember me."

Lillianna gasped. "You're the congressman who left me fifty dollars!"

"Ah, now you remember." He looked around at the others washing his car. "What's the car wash for?"

"Thomas, my beau." She lightly touched Tommy's forearm. "He needs money for cancer treatments."

The congressman frowned, then rubbed his chin. After he seemed to ponder for several seconds, his face brightened. "Hmm... I might have a proposition for you."

Lillianna and Thomas both inched closer.

"I know the Amish are hard workers and are good with children. I'm in desperate need of a nanny for my children and someone to do light housekeeping. If you agree to work for my wife and me for a year, I will pay Thomas' medical expenses."

Lillianna's jaw dropped. "You would pay for his treatments?"

"It would be a full-time, live-in job, so your room and meals are included. But my home is in Virginia. Does that sound like something you'd be interested in?"

Lillianna's face beamed. *This is an answer to prayer!*

Thomas spoke up. "Do you mind if we discuss this first?"

"Of course not. The decision is yours. Let me call my wife, though, to make sure she hasn't already found someone for the position."

Thomas pulled Lillianna to the side. "You don't have to do this, Lil."

"Tommy, he's going to pay for *all* your medical treatments."

"I know, but an entire year? I don't want you to give up an entire year of your life because of me."

"I would consider it an honor to do this for you, Tommy. I love you. I want you well. Besides, I love *kinner*. It wouldn't be a difficult job for me at all," she reasoned.

"What will your folks say?" He frowned.

She shrugged. "How else would we get the money? I think this is an answer from God. What else could it be?"

"A coincidence."

"Coincidence? You've got to be kidding. This is God, Tommy, and I think you *know* it."

He shrugged. "Think what you want. I admit that it's a great opportunity."

"What more would you like God to do for you, Thomas?"

He put a hand out to halt her words. "Not now, Lil."

"Okay, but I'm going to tell that man yes."

Thomas pasted on a fake smile. "Enemas, here I come. I can't believe I let you talk me into this."

Lillianna crossed her arms and frowned at him. "Thomas Girod," she warned.

"All right, let's go tell him."

Chapter Eleven

Lillianna's mind swirled with emotion as she thought of telling her folks what she had planned. What were they going to say? She gave the pot of soup one more stir, inhaling the delicious aroma, and placed it on the table along with a loaf of bread *Mamm* had made earlier this morning.

She glanced up and caught Tommy's wink when the family sat around the table. *Dat* said the prayer, and then each person began helping themselves to the nourishment in front of them. Lillianna's hands felt clammy knowing she needed to speak up. She wiped her hands on her dress and took a bite of bread to try to calm herself.

"How did the fund-raiser go today?" *Dat* asked.

Whew! This was the perfect time to tell her folks. "We didn't do very well, but a man came by." She glanced up at Thomas, then rushed on. "He made us a good offer."

Her father looked up. "Offer?"

She swallowed. "*Jah*, he asked what the car wash was for and we told him about Tommy's treatments. He said that if I come to work for him for a year, then he would pay for all of Thomas' medical expenses." Lillianna gave each of her folks a pleading look.

"A year is a long time. And you have your classes coming up," her mother said.

Her father glanced at Thomas and shook his head. "I don't think that is a good idea. You do not know this man."

"He is a congressman," she said.

Her father shook his head.

"But how else will we get the money?" Lillianna cried.

"I don't know." Her father shrugged.

"But *Dat*, Tommy needs his treatments now! He doesn't have a lot of time."

Dat gave her a look of warning. Raising one's voice was not permitted. "You have my answer."

She looked to her mother. "*Mamm*?"

"You heard what your father said."

Thomas spoke up, a look of resignation on his face. "Lil, it's okay."

"No, it's not okay. I'm not going to just let you die, Tommy! I won't do it." Lillianna pushed her chair back and ran out of the dining room. *How could* Mamm *and* Dat *be so uncaring? How could they just let Tommy die? Do they not care just because Tommy's* Englisch? She suspected her last thought to be the truth.

"Lil," Tommy approached the porch swing and sat down next to her. He took her hand in his.

"I'm going to do it anyway. They can't keep me here."

He chuckled. "Come here, my little warrior princess." Tommy pulled her close. "No one would ever mark you for a coward."

"I don't want to lose you." Lillianna sobbed. "I'm going to go work for Congressman Stevenson."

"I wish I knew some other way." He sighed, and then shot up when he had a thought. "I have an idea. Let's not wait, Lil. Let's get married now."

Lillianna's jaw dropped. "Married? Now?"

"Yes. We can marry next week and enjoy a whole week together before I go in for treatment. What do you say?"

"But you're not Amish."

"Neither are you. It's perfect." He paced the porch.

"But my family," she protested. "If I become *Englisch*, they'll shun me."

"Trust me, Lil. After you've been living in that *Englischer's* fancy house for a year, you're not going to *want* to go back to the Amish," he reasoned. "Besides, if you haven't joined the church, you won't be shunned. You know that."

"I know. It's just that…" She hung her head.

His exuberance deflated. "Lil, if you have no desire to marry me or you don't love me, please say so. If you—"

"No. You *know* I love you, Thomas. And I *want* to marry you. I'm just scared, I guess."

Thomas sat back down on the swing, next to Lillianna, and gathered her into his arms. "You have nothing to be scared of."

"How can you say that? You might die soon, Tommy!" She couldn't help the tear that trickled down her cheek.

"Well, look on the bright side. If I die, you can always join the Amish again. And you can remarry some Amish guy." He chuckled.

"I don't think that's funny, Thomas."

He lifted her chin and gazed into her troubled eyes. "If I live, we get to spend every day of our lives together, and maybe even have a family of our own someday. How does that sound?"

"Wonderful."

He smoothed her hair. "Lil, let's just take one day at a time. Today has enough problems of its own without us heaping on a bunch more. Don't borrow trouble, the interest is too high."

"You're quoting the Amish *and* the Bible? Hmm… maybe there's hope for you yet."

"I wouldn't hold my breath."

"No, you wouldn't. Because then you'll die and find out that there actually *is* a God Who you've been denying."

"Ouch, that wasn't nice."

"And not saying anything and allowing you to go to Hell is?"

"Enough. Point taken."

Lillianna sighed. "What am I going to do with you?"

"Marry me, hopefully?"

"I'm not ready yet, Thomas."

"Why?"

"Well, because. There are just so many things that we need to work through first. We don't believe the same things. I… I'm just not ready. If I marry, I need total peace about it."

"Will you please wait for me, then?"

"Of course. I already told you I would. Do you doubt my word?"

He shook his head. "Just worried, I guess. A lot could happen in a year. We'll be so far apart."

"Tommy, I can't imagine marrying anyone but you."

He bent down and pressed his lips to hers. "Nor I, you."

"I love you."

"I know. And I'm going to be dreaming about you every day that I'm gone."

Chapter Twelve

Carolanne and Samuel had returned from their trip to California last week. They'd had a wonderful *gut* time, Carolanne had said, but Lillianna detected weakness in her voice. Her once-vibrant skin seemed sallow; a sure sign her health was failing.

Lillianna wished with all her being that Carolanne would've tried the treatments Thomas would soon be undergoing, but she'd refused. She was certain her death was God's will and Lilly knew there was no way to change her mind. She'd tried to reason with her, and even talked to Samuel as well. He wished she'd do something too, but he let her have her way. Lillianna realized that Samuel would probably take Carolanne to the moon and back if that was what she wanted and he had the means to make it a reality.

Every day since they'd been home, Lillianna visited Carolanne. Each day it seemed that Carolanne's health grew worse. It wouldn't be long before her best friend was gone from this life. Since she knew these were Carolanne's final days, she'd called Congressman Stevenson and requested a later starting date. Fortunately, he'd agreed. From what Lillianna could see, he seemed like a compassionate man.

Lilly knocked on the door of the Beachy home and Samuel answered with a half-smile.

"She's not looking so well," he grimaced, permitting Lilly inside.

"I'm sorry, Samuel."

He swallowed and nodded.

Lillianna slowly walked to the bedroom with Samuel behind her. He pushed on the door and alerted Carolanne to their presence. She looked up from her bed and smiled. Samuel went near and kissed her forehead. "I'll be back after Lilly leaves, okay?"

Carolanne nodded.

He turned to Lillianna. "I'll be in the *schtupp* if you need me."

"Okay."

They both watched as Samuel walked out of the room.

Lillianna took Carolanne's hand. "How are you?"

"Not so *gut*, but I'll be better real soon." Carolanne gave a weak smile.

"I'm gonna miss you when you're gone. I wish you could stay." She sniffled.

Carolanne shook her head slightly. "I guess you won't be thinkin' on Samuel now that you've found your Thomas."

"*Nee*, I don't 'spect so."

"I am happy for you, but..." Carolanne grasped her other hand. "Lilly, if your Thomas does go, you and Samuel will need each other, *jah*?"

Lillianna nodded and an understanding passed between them. Knowing these were Carolanne's last moments, she felt like breaking down in tears. But Carolanne wouldn't want that. She'd said she didn't want to die in an atmosphere where everyone was sad, because there was only reason to be joyful. She wasn't really dying at all. She was passing from one home to another—one that was much more beautiful and magnificent than the one she currently inhabited. So why be gloomy?

Early the next day, Samuel stopped by the house and notified Lillianna that her friend had passed during the night.

The next few days seemed to go by in a flurry. She'd helped Carolanne's mother prepare the body for burial, an honor with which she was pleased to have been bestowed. She'd helped clean and prepare food for the event as well. Many Plain folk attended the funeral and several *Englischers* as well. Lillianna surmised that they had probably been Carolanne's customers at her bakeshop. *Jah*, her friend would be missed by many.

Poor Samuel seemed somber, as she'd expected. He'd begun pouring all his extra hours into his business, no doubt to take his mind off his wife's passing. It was a shame they didn't have any *kinner*, but she guessed that must've been the Lord's will. Perhaps Samuel wouldn't have been able to care for them on his own.

Lillianna recalled her promise to Carolanne on her deathbed. If Thomas didn't survive, she'd agree to become Samuel's wife. Now, she wished she had asked Carolanne if Samuel was privy to the idea. Had she asked Samuel the same thing? Did he have any idea what his wife had in mind for him? Lilly didn't think so.

An uncomfortable silence hung in the air as the family tended to the morning chores. Soon, Lillianna would be saying goodbye to her family. Most likely, she wouldn't be seeing them for an entire year. She couldn't help but feel a little nervous. What would it be like to be away from *Dat*, *Mamm*, and her five siblings who were still living at home? Aside from a couple of short trips, she'd been around her family every day of her life. It surely would be an adjustment.

She'd only been in a couple of *Englischers'* homes and felt ill at ease while visiting. Hopefully, the congressman's home would be different. Lillianna couldn't imagine becoming comfortable using electric, telephones, and computers regularly, and barely conversing with those around her. The whole idea seemed absurd.

She swept up the heap of debris on the floor, just prior to the boys and *Dat* marching in from outside chores. They removed their hats, washed up at the sink near the mudroom, and then took their places at the table. Lillianna quickly washed her hands as well and sat down. Her father bowed his head in silent prayer and the others followed suit.

Lillianna's mouth became dry. She felt like she should say something, but what? When would be the next time she shared a meal with her family?

"You aren't still planning to go work for that *Englischer*, are you?" Dat frowned.

She swallowed. "*Jah, Dat*. I have to. Thomas needs money for his treatments."

"You have already done what you could. Let *him* find the rest of the money."

"But he doesn't have time to wait. I have to go," she protested.

"I do not think this will be *gut* for you, *dochder*. Better to stay here and take your vows."

"No, *Dat*. I'm working for money for Thomas' treatments."

"You will go against my command?"

Lillianna wrung her hands. "I'm leaving at nine o'clock. They are coming to get me."

"If you insist on disregarding your father's and mother's words, you will not return home." Her father hadn't raised his voice, but he might as well have. His words pounded in Lillianna's ears.

Her eyes beseeched her mother's, but *Mamm* remained silent. She figured *Mamm* wouldn't go against *Dat's* word, but begged anyhow. *How can he*

force me to make this choice? "Fine. If you can't understand that Tommy needs me, then maybe I don't
want to come back home!" She threw her napkin on
the table and hurried to her bedroom. *I can't believe*
Dat's *shunning me.*

Two hours later, Lillianna left her childhood home
for good, with nary a goodbye from anyone. She
desperately hoped her sacrifice would be worth it.
It would simply be unbearable to endure this hard-
ship and lose Thomas as well.

Lillianna entered the limousine in shock. She felt
like breaking down in tears, but she couldn't. She'd
already shed so many over Carolanne's passing and
the situation with Thomas, it seemed her tears had
run dry. Either that, or she could only sustain so
much and her body was on overload.

She was literally entering a whole new world now,
full of forbidden things. She glanced around at the
fancy car's interior. *Jah*, this was a step up from a
horse and buggy. To her dismay, a window rolled
down revealing the interior of the front seat.

"My name is Jones," the driver informed her.

"Hello, Jones. My name is Lillianna."

He nodded in recognition. "The congressman said
to go ahead and enjoy some wine, which is in that
black cooler there, and relax. We've got a seven-hour
drive ahead of us."

"I don't drink wine, but *denki*."

"You'll also find other nonalcoholic drinks in

there, as well as snacks. Mr. Stevenson usually likes to keep it stocked. If you need anything from me, just push that button by the window. The television and radio remotes are inside the wooden console there. If you need a blanket or a pillow, you'll find them under the seat."

Lillianna nodded.

"And we'll be making a meal stop in a few hours." Jones looked up as though he were trying to recall if he'd missed anything. "I think that's about it." He smiled and the window rolled back up.

Butterflies filled Lillianna's stomach. This was all so exciting. Should she be excited, though? A feeling of guilt washed over her. How could she be happy right now with everything else going on around her?

She took a deep breath and pulled out her Bible. By providence, it opened to the book of Ecclesiastes, chapter three. She glanced down and read the words, "To every*thing there is* a season, and a time to every purpose under the heaven: A time to be born, and a time to die; a time to plant, and a time to pluck up *that which is* planted; A time to kill, and a time to heal; a time to break down, and a time to build up; A time to weep, and a time to laugh; a time to mourn, and a time to dance…" Lillianna closed her eyes and offered up a prayer of thankfulness. *Denki, Gott. You always know what I need and when I need it. You are so good. Help me to trust You more.*

Chapter Thirteen

Lillianna's eyes widened in anticipation as Jones pulled the limousine up to Congressman Stevenson's grand estate. She'd never visited a private home so fancy. A long wrought-iron fence enclosed the property, separating it from the rural road.

The entrance to the driveway screamed of wealth and prosperity. *Important government folks must make lots of money.* Lillianna inched closer to the window to take it all in. The long driveway, Jones had informed her, led up both sides of the grand courtyard lined with large oak trees. She guessed the mature trees to be over one hundred years old.

"All right, Miss Lillianna, here we are." Jones smiled as he held the door open for her departure. "I'll bring your bags up to the house."

"*Denki.*" She glanced around, wondering which door she should enter.

"Follow me," Jones instructed.

Lilly quietly followed behind Jones as he led the

way to the front entrance of the plantation-style home. She took in the sweeping front porch and turned back to gander at the great courtyard. *What a joy it would be to walk in the midst of the large oaks.* A sense of wonder filled her.

Jones punched some numbers into a panel and the door swung open. He confidently walked through the door and Lillianna followed. She looked behind the door and gaped in amazement when no one was there.

"Close front door," Jones said.

Lillianna watched in astonishment as the door closed on its own.

"Hello, Jones," a female voice called out of nowhere.

"Who is that?" Lillianna spoke up.

Jones chuckled. "It's a voice-activated facial-recognition security system. Mrs. Stevenson will have to program your name in too."

Lillianna just nodded, not wanting to admit her ignorance. She had no idea what he was talking about. This was fancier than anything she'd ever heard of.

A petite brunette entered the foyer. She smiled and offered Lillianna her hand. "You must be Lillianna."

Lillianna shook her hand and nodded.

"I am Candace, Clay's wife."

"*Gut* to meet you."

Candace turned to Jones. "Let's take those bags up to her room, Jones."

"Yes, Mrs. Stevenson." Jones lifted the bags.

"I'll show you to your room, Lillianna. We'll go over your duties tomorrow, as I'm certain you'd like to rest from your trip." Candace walked to a spiral staircase and Lillianna followed with Jones behind her.

"*Denki.*"

Candace came to a door and stopped. She turned the knob and opened the door to a beautiful, large bedroom. She turned to Jones. "You may leave those by the door. Thank you, Jones."

"Yes, Ma'am."

Lillianna briefly watched Jones descend the stairs, and then turned back to the wonderful *gut* room. Candace walked over to a door on the opposite side of the room. "This is your private bath and the closet is over there." She pointed to another door.

Lillianna opened the bathroom door and peered in. Her face brightened when she saw the giant bath tub. How lovely it would be to bathe this evening.

"Do you have any questions?" Candace asked.

Lillianna shook her head.

"Okay. Well, if you do, I'll be downstairs." Candace turned to go, and then turned back. "If you need to make any phone calls, there is a phone beside the bed. Feel free to use the computer as well. Everything in this room is for your use."

"*Denki.*"

"I'll leave you to get settled."

Lillianna watched Candace exit. She turned back

to her room, still disbelieving that she would be staying in a place so fancy. She walked to the window and peered out. An enormous flower garden was displayed below her. Many kinds of flowers, in a vast array of colors, seemed to weave through various green shrubberies. Several walking paths led to various places—one to a pond with a fountain of some sort in the middle, one to a grassy area where park benches and trees stood, and a couple more areas she couldn't see from her view. She'd have to check it out another day when there was more daylight available. *What a perfect place to read.*

She retreated from the window and whisked her bags to the closet. Her eyes bulged when she realized the closet was the size of a small room. *How much clothing does a fancy* Englischer *usually have? You can only wear one dress at a time.* Lillianna's closet at home was barely large enough to step into, but it was sufficient for her needs. She removed her shoes and placed them on one of the closet shelves, and then removed her second identical pair from her bag and placed them there too. After she finished emptying her clothing bag, she placed her personal items in the nightstand drawer next to the bed, and put her books onto an empty shelf in the bookcase.

Lillianna's bath had been relaxing, but she would've enjoyed it more if she hadn't been so tired. She quickly slipped into her nightgown and under the luxurious sheets of the impressive bed. She closed her eyes. *Thomas was right; I don't think I'll ever get used to being Amish again after the year is over.*

Lillianna padded downstairs, ready to start the day. The sun was barely rising and it appeared nobody had awakened yet. *A walk in the garden would be wonderful right now.* She quietly tiptoed to the door and gently pulled it open, so as not to wake anyone.

Suddenly a loud honking noise began, along with a strange high-pitched siren and flashing bright lights. Lillianna quickly closed the door and covered her ears. She'd never heard anything so frightening.

In short order, bare-chested Congressman Stevenson appeared in a pair of blue flannel pajama pants. He raced to the panel next to the door and quickly punched something in. Lillianna sighed when the house was finally silent again.

"I take it nobody's told you how to use the alarm system yet?" His arms crossed his chest.

Lillianna's cheeks burned as though she'd been standing too close to the cook stove. This was not how she'd envisioned starting out her new job. "*Ach,* no."

"Come here," he beckoned her close.

She felt uncomfortable being so near while he was standing shirtless.

"See those buttons? If no one is up and you'd like to leave the house, type in the passcode. For this door, it's six, two, seven, nine." He punched in the numbers.

"Six, two, seven, nine?"

He nodded. "Then you press the 'Disarm' button."

"Six, two, seven, nine, Disarm," she repeated, attempting to drill it into her brain.

"That's correct." He yawned. "I'm going back to bed now."

"Daddy, what was that noise?" a young boy asked from the bottom of the stairs.

The congressman whisked him up into his arms and tousled his hair. "*That* was the alarm. It's not time for you to get up yet, so go back up to your room. It should be quiet now." He set the boy down and gave his back a gentle pat.

Lillianna watched as the little boy made his way back upstairs.

"Good night," the congressman said as he journeyed toward his bedroom.

After all was quiet, Lillianna decided to postpone her waltz in the garden. She didn't want to take any chances of waking the household again. Instead, she headed back up to her room to read the Bible she'd brought along.

Chapter Fourteen

Lillianna was dying to make a large breakfast for the family, but she wouldn't without instruction first. After the humiliating incident this morning, she didn't dare take any chances. Who knows how many other strange things this fancy house was capable of? She sat on the love seat in the family room and waited for the Stevenson family to emerge from their rooms. She was really looking forward to meeting the *kinner*.

"Oh, wonderful! You're up." Candace walked into the family room with a child at each side.

"*Jah*. Would you like me to start making breakfast?" Lillianna stood up.

"That can wait a bit."

Lillianna glanced down at the small boy and girl. "Hello. Who are you?" She kneeled next to the youngest one.

The little one looked up at her mother, then hesitantly at Lillianna.

"You may tell her," Candace permitted.

The little girl hid behind her mother's leg.

"I'm Lillianna." She held her hand out to show her friendliness.

"She's going to be your new nanny," Candace explained.

The little boy spoke up. "Mommy, we don't need no nanny. We got you."

"It's 'we don't need *a* nanny'," she corrected. "And, yes, you do. Lillianna is going to watch you while Mommy and Daddy are gone."

"Does she make good food?" The boy eyed Lillianna undecidedly.

"If you tell her your name, I'll bet she'll make something for you." Candace raised her eyebrows.

The boy looked suspiciously at Lillianna and crossed his arms. "What will she make me?"

Lillianna glanced at Candace, who nodded. "Do you like coffee soup?"

"You're gonna make me coffee?" His eyes widened.

Lillianna nodded.

"I don't know about that." Congressman Stevenson entered the room.

Lillianna's excitement deflated.

"Yes, Daddy, coffee soup!" the boy protested.

"Offee thoup," his younger sister repeated.

The congressman raised an eyebrow at Lillianna. "Just what exactly is this coffee soup?"

"It's a little coffee, with mostly milk, and some sugar. We usually dip bread or crackers into it. It's quite tasty, actually. I've never met anyone who didn't like it."

"Coffee soup, coffee soup!" the two young ones demanded.

Candace spoke up, "It looks like you're outvoted, Clay."

He raised his hands in defeat. "I guess coffee soup, it is."

"Coffee soup!" the little ones chanted.

Lillianna put a hand on her hip. "Wait a minute. You haven't told me your names yet." She eyed the young ones.

"Calvin and Camille. She goes by Cammie, though, and I like Cal," the boy volunteered.

Lillianna smiled. "Nice to meet you, Cammie and Cal."

"Can we call ya 'Lilly'?" Cal asked.

"*May* we," his mother corrected.

"May we call ya 'Lilly'?" he asked again.

"'Lilly' is fine." She turned to Candace. "You'll have to show me how everything works here. I'm afraid this is much different than my Amish home."

"Of course. Follow me," Candace said. "Clay, will you keep the children out of the kitchen while Lillianna and I prepare breakfast?"

"Certainly," he said.

Lillianna followed behind Candace.

Upon entering the enormous kitchen, Candace pressed a button on the wall that lit up the entire room. Lillianna followed her employer around a large island to a flat black counter. "This is the stove top." Candace pressed another button that caused a red circular surface to appear. Lillianna put her hand over it and immediately felt the heat.

Candace pulled open a wooden panel that seemed like part of the cabinetry. "This is the oven." She turned and walked to the opposite side of the kitchen and opened another wooden panel. "This is the refrigerator. If you need to use any appliances, they're inside the island," Candace informed her.

"Island?" Lillianna's lips twisted.

Candace moved to the counter in the center of the kitchen. "This is the island." She smiled and opened one of the lower cabinet doors to reveal all kinds of gadgets.

Lillianna was certain she wouldn't be using any of those. "Where are the mixing bowls and wooden spoons?"

Candace opened up another cabinet. "Feel free to look around to find what you need. You saw the pots and pans, right?"

Lillianna looked up and pointed to a large cast-iron rack hanging from the ceiling. "Those?"

Candace nodded. "Any questions?"

"Where can I find the coffee and sugar?"

"The coffee will be in the freezer and the sugar is in a canister in the cupboard. The grinder is kept in the island." Candace removed the sugar, coffee, and the grinder and placed them on the island.

She opened up the bag and found wonderful-smelling beans inside. This was quite different than the coffee she was used to having. "I'm not sure how that works."

"It's simple. Remove the lid from the grinder and add some beans, close it and push down."

Lillianna did as instructed and jumped slightly when the grinder began.

Candace nodded satisfactorily and moved to join the others in the family room. "Oh, and I should warn you that Clay uses the kitchen often. He adores utilizing his culinary skills, so he'll probably prepare most of our dinners."

A man working in the kitchen? Yep, this was definitely a whole new world.

Chapter Fifteen

Thomas' arrival at the airport in San Diego had been pleasant enough, yet anxiety still prevailed concerning the treatments. He didn't think he'd ever be facing his cancer again. Prior to meeting Lillianna, he'd been resigned to his inevitable end. Finding Lillianna again had breathed new life into him. He now felt as though Mount Everest wouldn't be too difficult an obstacle. What other woman would've been willing to forfeit an entire year of her life for him? He *had to* get better, if for no other reason than for Lillianna.

As his eyes scanned the travelers, he looked for a sign with his name on it, as he'd been instructed to do. He eventually spotted a man with a baseball cap, holding a sign that read, "Thomas Girod". He quickly approached the man.

"I'm Thomas." He shook the man's hand.

"Tristan. Nice to meet you, Thomas." Tristan glanced down at his bag. "Do you have any checked luggage we need to pick up?"

Thomas shook his head. "Nope; this is it."

"Great. Let's get out of here." Tristan smiled.

As they drove near the border, Tristan informed Thomas of what to expect. "Is your passport handy? They don't always ask for it, but just in case."

Thomas nodded. Fortunately he'd acquired a passport a few months ago in anticipation of completing his "bucket list", the things he wished to do before he died. In fact, he probably wouldn't have seen Lillianna again, had it not been for his bucket list. The Grand Canyon was one of many places he'd wanted to see in the States before he traveled abroad. If all went well with his treatments, perhaps he and Lillianna would have the opportunity to travel. He smiled just thinking about it.

A yellow "caution" sign with a man, woman, and child running caught Thomas' eye. "What does that mean?"

"This is one of the busiest areas for illegal immigrant crossing. I heard they erected the signs after several people were struck by vehicles."

"Oh, wow." Thomas grasped his seat belt when traffic suddenly slowed to a near-stop.

"Whatever you do, don't give money to the street children," Tristan advised.

"Street children?"

"You'll see in just a little bit. They stand on the streets selling gum, candies, and other things. It's usually a lot worse on the way out because they have a captive audience with all the cars waiting in line to cross over the border."

"Why shouldn't we give to them?" Thomas felt like he could at least give a couple bucks to a needy child.

"If you give to one, they will all surround your car. Besides, it's dangerous for them to be weaving in and out of traffic, so I don't want to encourage it. It's a sad thing." As the border patrol waved them through, Tristan pointed. "See, there are some."

Thomas' eyes widened. "Those children can't be more than five or six years old! Who would allow their children to run around on the street like that?"

Tristan shrugged. "People think differently. Maybe they really need the money."

"I think I'd find a way to make money myself instead of sending my little ones off. Anyone could just pull them into their car and kidnap them."

"Sad. I know. And then there's human trafficking, where the poor children are sold to moneygrubbing men who prostitute them out to pedophiles." Tristan blew out a breath.

Thomas' skin crawled. "That's beyond belief."

"We often don't realize how good we have it, Thomas."

He nodded. "You're right. And I thought I was in a predicament with this cancer." Thomas grasped the door handle when another vehicle zoomed past and nearly ran them off the road. "Sheesh! The people drive crazy out here. I'll be lucky to even make it to the clinic."

Tristan chuckled. "I've been doing this for years and I'm still alive."

Thomas shook his head. "I don't see how."

"Only by the grace of God, is what I say."

Thomas knew he needed to change the subject quickly. The last thing he wanted was to begin another "God" conversation. "How'd you get this job?"

"My mother came here about twenty years ago for treatment. I saw how well these treatments work, in spite of all the negative press in the States, and I wanted to help out some way. My mother wasn't the only one getting well. Prior to coming here, she did her research. She talked with others who'd gone through it and compared their results with those who'd gone the traditional route. She realized the survival rate statistics in many of the Mexican clinics were much better than with conventional medicine. Sometimes I wonder about that, you know? You'd think if something works that the medical community would embrace it. The results these clinics get are impressive and I might not believe it had I not seen it with my own eyes. I admit I was skeptical at first."

"Why do you suppose these American cancer associations and doctors are so against it?" Thomas raised an eyebrow.

"One word: money. Think about it. The cancer industry is a multibillion dollar industry. What would happen if the answer to cancer was something simple—a plant that everyone could grow in their backyard?" Tristan pushed on the horn when another vehicle cut in front of him, nearly causing an accident.

"I'm not sure. I guess there would be a lot of people out of jobs."

"Bingo."

"So, what about your mother? Is she still alive?"

"My mom? Oh yeah, she's alive more now than ever. Once she began her treatments here, she only improved. She's been real good about only consuming what she's supposed to. The ones who stick with the diet and lifestyle are the ones who typically make it."

Thomas nodded. "That's what I've been told."

"Not everyone survives, of course. I believe that if it's your time to die, *no* treatment is gonna stop it. But if it isn't your time, your chances are a lot better here."

"Thank you. I feel a little more confident now. My fiancée talked me into this."

Tristan smiled. "You'll thank her later."

Tonight was the night they'd agreed on. Lillianna expected to receive Thomas' call. It would be the first since he'd gotten to the clinic. Even with all the activity in the house, Lillianna had become lonely. She desired to be there at the clinic with Thomas, offering encouragement. But he wouldn't even *be* at the clinic had it not been for Congressman Stevenson's generous offer. She must remember to thank him again.

Ten more minutes passed by and Lillianna yawned. She glanced at the clock and noticed it was an hour past her typical bedtime. If Tommy didn't call soon, she'd fall asleep.

Thomas sighed as Tristan, his chauffeur and now friend, drove away. He was definitely charting new waters here in this foreign land. Two things he'd immediately noticed were the presence of poverty and the abundance of color. No plain white farm houses like in Pennsylvania. In truth, he was beginning to feel homesick—not a good sign when there were many months of treatment ahead.

Well, here I go, for better or worse. He opened the door of the treatment center and was instantly greeted by attentive friendly smiles. He was pleasantly surprised when he entered the building. The atmosphere looked very much like an American hospital; it was professional, yet felt less sterile and emanated more of a homey feel. Immediately, his mind was set at ease and he strode to the front desk with confidence.

Chapter Sixteen

Lillianna quickly fixed the children's breakfast and placed a plate on the bar for each of them. She walked to the wood-encased black chalkboard and read the list of duties she was to perform. Today would be a full day. She'd escort Calvin and Camille to their various activities—Camille to gymnastics and Calvin to karate. When their activities were completed, she was to make a grocery shopping trip, and then stop at the dry cleaners to pick up the Stevensons' laundry.

The congressman and his wife had a charity event to attend, so they most likely wouldn't be returning until late this evening.

Lillianna grinned when she heard the telephone ringing upstairs. *Thomas.* Her heart thrilled every time she heard the sound. It was like church bells ringing during Christmastime, chiming favorite hymns of the Nativity of Christ. She immediately rushed upstairs to answer. It was times like this that she wished her room wasn't the only one to have a phone. Of course, she could have just brought the cordless receiver downstairs but she had an awful habit of forgetting where she'd put things.

"Thomas?" She was certain he heard the excitement in her voice.

"Sorry to disappoint you. This is Clay Stevenson."

"Oh, sorry, Congressman. I thought it was someone else." She cleared her throat.

"Yes, I gathered that." He chuckled. "My reason for calling is that we'd like you to have the children ready to go at five. Candace would like them to be present at the charity gala this evening. Calvin has a tuxedo in his closet and there is a red gown in Camille's. They'll know which shoes to wear."

She mentally counted the available hours. Would there be enough time? "Okay."

"It would be good if you would come along as well."

Lillianna's jaw dropped. "Me?"

"Don't worry; Candace has plenty of party dresses in various sizes that would be suitable for the occasion. She keeps extras on hand just in case."

An Englisch *dress?* "But I—"

"Excuse me, I've gotta go. See you there." He clicked off abruptly.

Lillianna stared at the receiver in her hand while a buzzing noise sounded from the other end of the line. *I can't wear an* Englisch *dress, can I? What would* Dat *think?* She suddenly heard the *kinner* downstairs and remembered their appointments. If they were going to make it on time, they needed to leave promptly. She'd worry about the dinner at a later time.

Thomas held the phone to his ear as it rang and rang. *Where's Lil?* He reluctantly hung up the phone, chiding himself for not calling last night when she'd expected him to. He'd have to try again this evening.

He turned at a knock on the door. "Come in."

An administrator appeared. "How do you like your accommodations?"

"Oh, they're great. A lot better than what I'd envisioned."

The administrator laughed. "You're not the first one to say that. A lot of patients are pleasantly surprised when they come here. I guess the media paints a pretty bad picture of the clinics here."

Thomas recalled what Tristan had said. "I've heard."

"Don't get me wrong. Just like in the U.S., there are good and bad doctors. Some genuinely want to help people and others practice for less-than-desirable reasons. But the majority of natural clinics are here because they want the treatments to be easily accessible for North Americans. They'd practice in the States if they didn't fear the powers-that-be confiscating their possessions and putting them in jail."

"Jail? Really?"

"It's a tricky problem, actually. If a doctor wants

to practice natural medicine and use treatments that '*the authorities*' say are 'unapproved' or 'ineffective', they are blacklisted as 'quacks'. The AMA will strip them of their licenses and charge them for 'practicing medicine without a license'."

"That hardly seems fair." Thomas rubbed his forehead.

"Maybe so, but that's the way it is."

"You'd think there'd be more medical freedom in America and they'd let the people *choose* which treatments they'd like to pursue."

"You'd think so, huh? Nope. There have even been several people *forced* to undergo chemotherapy against their wishes."

"Oh man, I couldn't imagine. I think I might have heard something about that, now that you mention it. Wasn't there an Amish girl taken away from her parents?"

"Yep. There have been many children forced against their own and their parents' wishes. I've heard it called 'gunpoint medicine'. Sad, but true. It's kind of scary. It reminds me of the days of Hitler and how people were forced to do whatever the government commanded. He's even quoted as saying, 'If you tell a lie loud enough, long enough, and often enough, the people will believe it' and 'People are more likely to believe a big lie than a small one.' I'm afraid our people have believed some really big lies."

"Wow. That *is* a scary thought." Thomas shuddered.

"Well, we can dwell on the negatives or we can do our best to stay positive. We need to get you well. That way, you can go share your experience and shed a little light in the darkness."

"I agree. Do you really think this is going to work?"

"We've seen amazing results here. I'm not going to promise anything. God's the only one who knows how many days each of us has. But the odds are in your favor if you follow the doctors' advice."

Thomas nodded in understanding.

"Your lab work is ready and the doctors are ready to discuss your treatment."

"Great. Let's go kick this thing."

The administrator chuckled. "That's what we like to hear."

Honestly, Lillianna didn't feel like attending the charity gala. Being in a room full of fancy *Englisch* strangers was not her cup of tea. Aside from being exhausted from the day's activities, she worried about what she would wear. She preferred to wear her cape dress, but Clay had insisted she wear something from Candace's closet.

As she stood in the large closet, she gaped at all the fancy gowns. It seemed as though she kept dresses in several sizes; perhaps for guests? She searched for something in her own size, although she didn't know which size that was. All her clothing had always been handmade. She pulled out a few dresses that looked like they might fit. One was red—she immediately put that one to the side knowing she'd never be comfortable in a dress that color. The blue and green gowns stared back at her. One of them, the green one, was strapless. It wouldn't do at all. Conversely, the blue dress had a slit that began at the thigh. That one wouldn't do either.

Her eyes moved back to the red gown. It appeared to be the most modest of the three. It would have to do. What other choice did she have? She hurriedly tried the dress on. When she glanced into the mirror, her jaw went slack. She'd never bared her arms, or her figure, in public. Lillianna pulled at the dress to see if it would loosen any. What would *Dat* and *Mamm* think if they saw her in this? She immediately pushed the thought out of her mind. She didn't have time to dwell on what-ifs. Jones would be there any moment to pick them up.

Lillianna quickly picked out a pair of shoes that would fit. Those weren't any more comfortable than the dress. At that moment, she promised herself she would never complain about her practical plain clothes again. They may not be the fanciest, but at least they were comfortable. After removing her prayer *kapp*, she brushed her hair and pinned it up neatly in a bun.

Lillianna sat at the table with the *kinner* on each side of her. They watched with delight as the congressman and his wife graced the dance floor. *They make a nice couple.* Lillianna smiled. *What would it be like to dance with Thomas?* She briefly wondered if she'd ever have the opportunity. *Please let it be so,* Gott. *Please let Thomas get well.*

Prior to the dance floor opening, they'd had two auctions, one silent and one live. The event helped to put her mind at ease some. She'd attended many auctions growing up and that familiarity produced a calm in her soul. But that calm was replaced with sadness when she realized that she no longer had a home. *Dat* had said to never return.

She'd been dumbfounded when she heard some of the items being auctioned off. A ride in an F-16 fighter jet, a ride on the track with a famous race car driver, and a three-day cruise were just a few of the top-dollar items. Clay Stevenson bid the highest on the last item, to the delight of his wife. Apparently, Candace had always wanted to go on a cruise. Lillianna had no idea why being stuck on a ship for three days would be appealing to anyone. Nevertheless, she was happy for Candace.

When the Stevenson adults returned to the table, Candace asked Lillianna if she'd ever danced. Of course, her answer was no. Candace leaned over to Clay and whispered in his ear. Clay scooted his chair out and walked over to Lillianna.

"May I have this dance?" He held out his hand.

Lillianna felt her temperature rise. "Oh no, I—"

"I insist." He smiled.

"Dance, dance," the *kinner* chanted.

She looked to Candace, who nodded.

"Well…okay," she acquiesced.

Clay led her out onto the center of the dance floor. "Never danced before?"

She shook her head.

"Okay, here's what you do." He grasped her left hand. She was certain it felt clammy. "This hand goes on my shoulder, here." He took her other hand in his and raised it midair. "And this hand, like so."

Lillianna gulped when she felt his other hand wrap around her waist. Other than Thomas, she'd never been this close to any man. This was awkward. She looked back to the table at Candace and the children. They smiled and waved.

"Now, take a deep breath and relax."

She did as he instructed.

"Good. Now just move your feet to the music and follow me."

Clay and Lillianna moved across the dance floor several times as the music played. She never realized how intimate dancing was. It was definitely something that should only be performed between married couples, she decided.

"You look very nice in that dress." Clay interrupted her thoughts. "Red is a good color for you. You should wear it often."

She felt heat rising to her cheeks again. "Where I come from, it is *verboten*."

"I'm sure your boyfriend would really like it." His eyes swept over her figure once again.

"I—uh we should probably stop now." She became flustered.

He smiled. "Just as soon as the song is over. Relax."

Lillianna was happy when the song finally ended. She did appreciate Clay teaching her how to dance, but it seemed...*wrong* somehow. Besides that, her feet were aching to get out of the shoes she wore. One thing she knew for sure: she would sleep *gut* this night.

Chapter Seventeen

"Lilly, Clay and I would like to invite you to join us and the children for church," Candace said, over her breakfast plate.

Lillianna glanced up at the clock. Eight-thirty. "What time does it begin?"

"They have several services. We've already missed the first one. The second one begins at nine-thirty, and the third starts at eleven."

"*Jah*, I'd like to go. Do you think it is okay to wear my cape dress?" She hoped Candace would say yes.

"Oh, yeah. Just wear whatever you'd like. Some people dress up in nice clothes. Others wear shorts and tank tops. Everyone is welcome."

Shorts and tank tops? Lillianna had always been taught to wear her *for gut* dress to meeting, the nicest she had. She briefly wondered if they would also allow someone in a two-piece bathing suit.

* * *

Lillianna stared up at the words on the large screen. She found keeping up with the tempo of the songs difficult. She was used to singing ancient hymns at a rate of ten seconds per syllable. This was quite a contrast.

She covertly glanced around at the other attendees. There were several young people talking, one girl was applying lip gloss, and several young men seemed to be checking out the young women in the short skirts. And many of the people stared at her in her Amish clothing. She felt like staring right back at them, but she wouldn't. She'd been taught how to behave properly during meeting. She couldn't imagine Amish young folks behaving like these worldly *Englischers*.

The sermon had been entertaining and she'd been surprised there was only one. She'd become a little confused, though, when the pastor read the "Bible" from his notes. What he read sounded nothing like what her Bible said. Instead, it sounded as though he were reading a novel or a motivational book of some sort.

When the service ended two hours earlier than her normal Amish meeting would have, they shook hands and Candace introduced her to some of her church friends. They all joined together in a large room where refreshments were served. Lillianna found the entire experience interesting, but she felt so out of place. Was this the way all *Englisch* church meetings went? She'd have to ask Candace about that later.

Thomas had been reluctant, but eventually gave in to the invitations of his patient-friends and, at their encouragement, he attended their Sunday meeting. He hadn't attended any type of religious service since he'd left the Amish over three years ago.

He admitted that the reason he attended was for purely selfish reasons. If Lillianna agreed to marry him, he was going to have to have some type of religious influence in his life. He could stand attending a meeting once a week if Lillianna was by his side. He would do it for her.

He was one of about thirty who attended. One of the doctors brought his guitar along while the others sang. Well, everyone except him. He sat through most of the meeting with his arms crossed. It was all a joke, as far as he was concerned. He didn't buy any of this religious stuff.

Thirty minutes later, he was glad the service was over. He longed to see Lillianna, to hold her in his arms. But for now, a phone call would have to do.

"Do you know anything about evolution?" Lillianna asked Candace as they walked side by side in the garden. The children played just up ahead of them on a swing set.

"Some...what do you want to know about it?"

"Do you believe in it?"

"Me?" Candace shook her head. "No. I never have. I always thought the idea that all life came from a single cell was preposterous. There's too much complexity in nature to not believe in a Creator."

"How would a person be able to show some-one that evolution isn't true?" Lillianna spoke her thoughts.

"That's a tough one. Does this person claim to be an atheist?"

"*Jah.* He says he doesn't believe in God."

"I usually find that there's a deeper reason that people refuse to believe in God. A lot of times there's been a tragedy in their lives, something they can't make sense of, and they blame God for it. As a con-sequence, they turn away from God as a sort of pun-ishment. They somehow think they're getting back at God by refusing to believe in Him, when they know in their hearts that He's real." Candace pulled Ca-mille's swing back and released it. "Either that, or they want to live a life of sin and don't want to have to account for the way they live."

"I think that's what happened to Thomas, my beau. He says he doesn't believe in God, but I think maybe he blames God for his folks' death."

"He'll need to work through his grief, I think. Losing a parent can be very traumatic for a child," Candace sympathized. "You can help him work through that."

Lillianna nodded. "I hope so."

"You know, if I recall correctly, I watched some

videos online that someone recommended to me on Facebook. They were really good. I think the man's name was Kent Hovind. He's a Creation Scientist. You're welcome to use that computer in your room to look him up."

"Oh, I've never used a computer. I wouldn't know how."

"It's not difficult. I can show you if you'd like."

"I would appreciate that." Lillianna smiled. Finally, she'd have some answers for Tommy.

Lillianna quickly snatched up the phone on the second ring. "Hello?"

"How's my beautiful girl doing today?" Thomas' voice caused her heart to flip-flop.

"I am *gut*. How are you?"

"Treatment is going better than expected. Guess what?"

"What?"

"No enemas."

Lillianna laughed. "Was that your biggest concern?"

"Mostly. You won't believe it here, Lil. The people are so easygoing. The doctors laid out the different treatment options, which are all natural by the way, that would work best for my cancer and *I* got to choose which treatments I want to use." She easily picked up the excitement in his voice.

"That sounds wonderful, Thomas. How are you feeling?"

"All right. I'm adjusting to the different foods and juices and things, so my body is a little wacky right now. They said that's normal, though. Once my body has a chance to cleanse itself, it can begin rebuilding the damage caused by the cancer and chemo."

"Glad to hear it." She hesitated. "I miss you."

"I miss you too, Lil. I can't wait until this is over and you and I can begin our lives together. How is it going at the Stevenson place?"

"Fine. I went to church on Sunday."

"An *Englischers'* church? Really?"

"*Jah.* It was awkward."

"I know what you mean. I attended a service here on Sunday too," he admitted.

"You did, Thomas?" She was certain he heard the surprise in her voice.

"I wish I hadn't."

Her joy deflated. "Oh."

"I shared a meal afterward with one of the patients who attended. Some Bible-thumper. Do you know he had the audacity to call me a liar to my face?" She heard Thomas' ire.

"Why?"

"Because I told him that God doesn't exist."

Lillianna took a deep breath and prayed for words of wisdom. "Thomas, you know I love you, but I need to say something."

"Okay."

"Every time someone reaches out to you, even if it's to point out your sin and they seem to be judging you, it is a token of God's mercy. He sees the past, present, and future. Jesus is the only way to Heaven: the Way, the Truth, and the Life. He is your *only* hope. He is your Creator and He loves you more than you could ever love yourself. Please turn to Him. Please don't be deceived into thinking your way is better than His. God's way is perfect."

"Wow, Lil. I didn't know you'd become a preacher." He chuckled.

"Thomas," she warned.

"I'm kidding, baby. I'm trying; I really am. That's why I went to the service on Sunday. But please don't start telling me that I'm going to Hell."

Tears rushed to Lillianna's eyes. "I don't know what to do or say to you, Tommy. You're about to die. I don't see how you *can't* be thinking about these things."

"I didn't say I haven't thought about it. I just need to work through things my own way. Understand?"

Lillianna shrugged her shoulders as though Tommy could see her through the phone. "Guess so." She remembered what Candace had said earlier. "Tommy, do you have a computer there?"

"A computer? Yeah, I brought my laptop along. Why?"

"Well, would you be willing to watch something? Candace told me about a man who has some videos online. She said they were really *gut*. Would you give them a try?"

"What are they about?"

"Evolution and Creation. And before you say no, remember *you're* the one who said to keep an open mind."

He chuckled. "Okay, you win. I'll check them out."

"*Denki*, Tommy."

Chapter Eighteen

Lillianna's face brightened when a gentle knock rapped on her door. *Must be one of the* kinner. She'd quickly fallen in love with young Cammie and Cal and felt as though she were more of an aunt to them rather than a nanny. Since Candace only worked part-time, today was one of the days Lillianna didn't have to tend to the children's needs.

"*Kumm*," she invited.

The two children rushed in and abruptly jumped onto the bed. Calvin handed Lillianna a letter.

"A letter for me?" Lillianna's brow rose.

"Yep, Mommy said we could bring it to you," Cammie informed her.

"Who's it from?" Cal asked.

Lillianna noticed the address right away. *Home.* "My younger sister." She determined by the handwriting.

"Do you want us to leave so you can read it?" Cal asked.

"No, I can read it later. You two can stay for a while." Lillianna walked to the desk in her room and tucked the letter into her Bible.

Calvin looked around her room and frowned. "Must be boring in here with no toys."

Lillianna chuckled. "I imagine for a five-year-old it might be boring. Do you like to read?"

"I read!" Cammie handed her a board book with no words.

Lilly smiled. "You do, don't you? Will you read to me?"

Cammie's eyes grew wide and she nodded vigorously. She sidled up close to Lillianna, then eventually climbed into her lap. Lillianna loved the smell of Camille's freshly-shampooed hair.

"Pincess loves horsey. Horsey loves Pincess." Cammie flipped a couple of pages. "Bad guy wants to take horsey from Pincess."

Lillianna smiled when she saw that the "bad guy" was actually the handsome prince. Children's imaginations were wonderful.

"Calvin, Camille," Candace called from downstairs.

"Oh, Mommy's calling. You better go now." Lillianna helped Calvin and Camille off the bed.

"I wanna read!" Cammie pouted.

"*Nee*, you must obey your mother. Go now. You can finish reading that to me later."

Camille's face brightened. "Okay."

Lillianna watched as the children exited her room.

Camille's book was tucked securely under her arm and Calvin marched like a soldier. She yearned for the day she and Tommy would marry and they would have *kinner* of their own. She briefly wondered what they would look like. Would they favor her or Tommy or be a mixture of both?

Time to read Mandy's letter. She pulled the envelope from her Bible and sank into the comfy office chair near her desk.

Dear Lilly,

Greetings in the name of our Lord. I hope this letter finds you well. Mamm *says to tell you hello, but she won't be writing to you. I think you already know why.* Dat *doesn't allow any of us to mention your name. He doesn't know that I'm writing to you. He's certain you're headed for Hell since you disobeyed him and are living at the* Englischers' *house.*

I have happy news. James and I are getting hitched come wedding season. I wish you could be here for it. Mamm *and* Dat *don't know yet, but they will find out before too long.*

How is Thomas? Have you heard from him? How are you doing in that fancy Englischer's *house?* Dat *about fainted dead away when he saw that fancy car pull up. I kind of wished it were me going instead. How exciting to live an* Englisch *life for a whole year! But you'll come back to the Amish, won't you, Lilly? I hope so*

'cause I don't like seeing Mamm *and* Dat *this way. They are praying hard for you. I hope you'll write me back.*
Your favorite sister (haha),
Mandy

Lillianna folded the letter up and placed it back into the envelope, then tucked it into her Bible. She'd send a letter back tomorrow.

Lillianna savored the chicken fajita supper Clay had prepared for the family. He really was a great cook, to Lilly's surprise. Apparently, before his political career he'd tried his hand in the culinary arts. His schooling paid off well, she admitted. She'd have to ask him what kind of spices he used.

Clay hopped up from the dinner table. "Oh, I almost forgot." He went to his briefcase and pulled out a tabloid newspaper. He thrust it toward Candace. "You're not going to believe this. Frank brought this to me today. He found it at the grocery store."

Candace held the paper up to read it. "Oh, my. How can they say that?"

Lillianna had no clue as to what they were talking about but figured it wasn't any of her business.

"You've gotta see this, Lillianna." Candace handed her the newspaper.

Lilly stared down at a photograph of herself dancing with Clay Stevenson. She read the title, "*Congressman Stevenson in the Embrace of Mysterious*

Woman". She continued to read the story which hinted at them having an affair. Her mouth dropped. "How can they write such lies?"

Candace shrugged. "It's the media—sensational journalism—they make up whatever they want to. They don't care if it's true or not."

"But that's wrong," she protested.

"That's life. Don't worry, most people won't believe it. You can't trust anything those tabloids write," Clay said. He reached over and gently rubbed her hand in reassurance.

Lillianna shook her head in disgust. *Dat would surely believe it if he saw it. And what about Thomas?* It looked like she would be doing a lot of praying tonight.

"By the way, Lillianna, do you think you can handle a weekend off? We were planning on getting away one of these weekends." Candace leaned over and whispered, "We want to take the kids someplace special."

A whole weekend off? What would she do with herself? She immediately began planning and a smile turned up the sides of her lips.

Sure enough, Thomas had seen the paper. She'd hoped to spare him the grief, but she could only control so much. Hopefully, Tommy trusted her enough to know she'd never do something like what they'd mentioned in the fake article.

"I believe you, Lil. But help me understand why

you're in the arms of Congressman Stevenson. In a very appealing dress, I might add." Thomas' disillusioned voice rang clear.

She realized she owed him an explanation. "I didn't want to go. I didn't want to wear the dress. And I really didn't even want to dance. I felt compelled to. It was Candace who suggested it because I'd said I'd never danced before. She and the *kinner* were at the table watching the whole time. It was a charity auction."

"If you say that's what happened, I believe you. I just don't want anyone stealing my girl while I'm gone."

"If I was going to sleep with anyone, it would've been with you. Not some married politician."

"Hey, I like the sound of that! I think I'll ask them to up my vitamin C dosage so I can get home quicker." He chuckled.

"*After* we're married," she emphasized.

"I'm counting the days." She could see his smile through the phone.

Chapter Nineteen

Lillianna hopped up when the doorbell rang and hurried toward the door. It was most likely another package, which the Stevenson family seemed to receive often.

"Keep playing, but wait when it comes to my turn," she instructed Camille and Calvin.

She yanked the door open.

"Oh… Samuel?" Lillianna said in surprise.

"Hiya, Lillianna. I, uh, brought something for you." Samuel Beachy held a quilt under one arm. He rubbed the back of his neck and looked away quickly.

Lillianna's heart went out to him. She really didn't know what to say to Carolanne's widower. "How are you doing?"

He gave a slight nod. "I have something of Carolanne's." His eyes shifted downward and he swallowed. "I hope you don't mind me coming here. You were a *gut* friend. I thought you would like to have this quilt."

"*Denki*, Samuel. But are you sure you don't want to keep it?"

"I kept one. I'm leaving for Pennsylvania soon. I decided to go back home." His eyes brightened a little at the mention of home.

She nodded in appreciation and received the quilt from his outstretched arms. "I hope you'll be happy there, Samuel."

He nodded and turned to go.

"Uh, Samuel," she called out.

He stopped and turned around.

"Thank you for loving Carolanne. You were *gut* for her. She couldn't have found a better husband."

He raised a half-smile. "*Denki.*"

Lillianna watched as Samuel drove away in a vehicle chauffeured by an *Englisch* driver. With all her heart, she wished Samuel the best. Perhaps he could find love again in Pennsylvania.

For the first time since his diagnosis, Thomas felt hopeful. New possibilities danced in his mind as he realized he might actually have a *future*. A future with Lil, a future with...his siblings? He hadn't thought much about it, but what if he and Lil went back to Pennsylvania? She'd said that her father had shunned her, so that door was pretty much closed. Not that they would be joining the Amish church anyway. No way.

Thomas pondered the idea for a few more moments, then finalized his decision. He'd send a letter to his sister, Rhoda.

"Hey." Michael, a fellow patient, popped his head in the door. "Some of us are heading to the beach. Wanna come?"

"Ah, can't, man. I've got an IV treatment in a half hour," Thomas declined. "Thanks for the invite, though."

"No, prob. Maybe next time."

Thomas had been to the beach twice already. The water had been pleasant and the beach was beautiful, although he had to be mindful of the jellyfish. And the women in bathing suits. He briefly imagined what Lillianna would look like in one. Would he ever get her to wear one? He sure hoped so.

He glanced up at the clock on the wall and determined he'd still have enough time to write that letter before his next treatment session started. He'd better get busy.

Lillianna scanned over the checklist Candace had given her. Had she packed everything the *kinner* needed for their trip? She opened up their suitcases one more time, making sure she hadn't missed anything. She wouldn't want the Stevensons to be disappointed in her childcare skills. Who knows? Perhaps they'd want her to work for them again in the future. She was certain she and Thomas could use the extra money after they were wed.

The Stevensons had been generous in giving her

an entire weekend off. She'd never had that much time to herself and she briefly wondered what she'd do. Certainly, she'd think of something.

Chapter Twenty

Lillianna awoke with a smile, realizing she had the next two days to herself. She walked into the restroom and glanced down at the fancy bathtub. *This is the perfect time to indulge in a bubble bath.* She turned the water on, poured in some bubble bath, and let it run until it was half full.

She giggled. This would be fun. Nothing much to do except enjoy herself and be lazy all day. Of course, she had her list of daily chores to do but those would only take a few hours at the most. She'd have plenty of time to complete them later. First a bath, then a phone call to Thomas, and the videos Candace had recommended. Maybe she'd make some zucchini bread too.

Lillianna quickly slipped out of the clothes she'd worn to bed, removed her sleeping *kapp*, and let her hair down. She peered into the bubbly water and dipped her foot in. *Ouch!* She'd made it too hot. She'd have to wait a bit before slipping in. Opening up the

medicine cabinet above the sink, she found the body
wash and shampoo and placed them near the tub.
Candles! Lillianna remembered the candles Candace
had generously offered to let her use. She'd have to
go get them from the master bathroom towel closet.

A cup of tea sounds gut. Lillianna snatched her
robe from off the hook in the bathroom and hastily
wrapped it around her. She'd have plenty of time
to make a cup of tea and get the candles before the
bathwater cooled down. Lillianna filled the kettle
and heated the water; she poured it into a mug and
dropped a tea bag in to steep.

Lillianna took a sip of the hot beverage and placed
it on a dresser in Candace's room. She opened the
towel closet and searched for the tea light candles,
recalling that Candace said they were on the top
shelf. She removed several small boxes of candles
and smelled each one. *Vanilla, mmm...* She took the
box of vanilla candles and placed the others neatly
back on the shelf.

A nearly inaudible squeak drew her attention to
the congressman's office door. *Oh no, is someone in
there?* She hastily picked up her teacup and started
toward her room.

"No need to run off, it's just me," the congressman's voice called from his office door.

"*Ach*, I thought you'd left. I didn't realize anyone
was here." Lillianna glanced down at herself in a
robe and her cheeks flushed.

"I had a little business to finish up, so I sent the

family on ahead. I plan to meet up with them this evening." He stepped toward her and smiled. "It's just the two of us here."

"I'll get out of your way, then. My bath is getting cold." Lillianna felt more awkward by the minute.

The congressman quickly stepped in front of her, blocking the path. "Your hair is beautiful down." He reached out and stroked her hair with his fingers. "You should wear it this way all the time."

"I need to go." Lillianna's pulse quickened.

"What's your hurry?" He grasped the teacup from her hand and moved it to the dresser.

Lillianna rapidly made her way toward the door, but it closed just before she reached it. She twisted the doorknob to no avail. What was going on?

The congressman roared with laughter and held up a remote control. "Thought you'd get away that easily?"

"Please, Congressman Stevenson, stop playing games."

"Oh, this is no game. And call me Clay, please. Congressman Stevenson sounds so…impersonal," he said nonchalantly.

"Please open the door, Clay." She twisted the knob again, attempting to escape.

"I will. Eventually." He stuck the remote control under his pillow and advanced toward Lillianna. He brought his hand to her face and gently caressed her cheek and neck. "You know, you looked really se-ductive in that dress you wore to the charity gala."

"Take your hand off me!" She swiftly batted his hand away and desperately searched for a way of escape. She could lock herself in the bathroom. Lillianna rushed to the bathroom with all her being.

"You won't get away." Clay caught her arm. "Come on, baby, let's have some fun."

"This isn't fun!" Lillianna couldn't suppress the tears that surfaced. "Please, let me go."

"I'm afraid I can't do that. But I can promise you this; you'll enjoy this much more if you just relax a little bit." He kept a grip on one arm and pulled her to the bed.

"No. I'm marrying Thomas! He will—"

"*If* he makes it home alive—and that's a big if—Thomas will never know. Unless, of course, you tell him." He bent down and whispered in her ear, his breath hot on her neck. "This will be our little secret, just between you and me."

She squirmed under his grasp and frantically thought of something to say to persuade him otherwise. "But your wife. She'll find out. I'll tell her."

"And lose all your precious money for Thomas' treatments?" He clicked his tongue. "We both know you're much smarter than that. Besides, you and Candace are such good friends now. You'd hate to throw that friendship away. And she'll never take your word over mine."

"I'll tell the police! You'll go to jail." She squirmed as he leaned in against her, pinning her between his body and the comforter.

"Now, now. And here I thought you were a nice Amish girl. Even so, that might be difficult to do since I know all the lawmen and judges around here. Besides, they all have their mistresses too." He rubbed his chin. "Hmm... I could probably have *you* arrested, though."

Lillianna gasped. "Me? What for?"

He shrugged his shoulders. "Hmm... I don't know. How does theft sound?"

"But I haven't stolen anything. I wouldn't."

"Oh, how naïve you Amish girls are." He quickly removed his shirt, then bent down and kissed her on the mouth.

Lillianna spit in his face and once again struggled to get free.

Clay wiped the saliva off his cheek. "Have it your way." His hand flew across Lillianna's cheek causing a sharp sting. "I wanted to play nice, but it seems like you want to fight. Let's kiss and make up?"

"Please, let me go," Lillianna broke down in tears. "Don't do this!" she cried in desperation.

"There, there, now." He wiped away one of her tears. "I didn't want to hit you but you gave me no choice. Just relax, baby. I promise it won't be so bad. You might actually enjoy it. The quicker you unwind, the sooner we'll be done and I can go meet my family."

Lillianna attempted to push him off of her, but she was no match for his strength. She frantically wrestled for several moments, trying to break free, but he continued to advance. Exhausted physically and emotionally, she didn't possess the energy to keep up the struggle.

"That's right. Smart girl."

No! Please, no.

Lillianna had never hated anyone in her life, but at this moment she found loving her enemy impossible.

Thomas couldn't shake the feeling of foreboding. Something wasn't quite right, although he had no clue what it was. Was it Lil? He rapidly picked up the phone and dialed the number. It rang continually, but no one ever answered. Perhaps Lil was outside? He'd have to try again later.

Lillianna shook like a leaf in the wind, clinging to the tree for dear life. Her eyes popped open and she realized where she was—in Clay Stevenson's bed. She hoped she'd just had a nightmare, but the evidence testified otherwise. Remembering the struggle hours before, she began sobbing again. Life would never be the same after this. Never.

She quickly sat up and the sheet slipped off her bare body. Lillianna hastily grabbed the sheet and protectively covered her body again. She looked for the robe she'd been wearing earlier and spotted a note on the pillow next to her. It bore the congressman's handwriting. *Thanks for the good time. Until next time, Clay.*

Until next time? Lillianna crumpled the note, threw it at the wall, and screamed.

Chapter Twenty-One

Lillianna heard Candace and the children's voices downstairs. *Oh, how she'd been dreading this day!* It had been just two days since the act. Two grueling horrible days of pain and loneliness. She wasn't ready to face the world yet. Would she ever be ready?

She'd have to get out of bed now to attend to the family's needs. No doubt they would have oodles of laundry. And they'd expect supper. Just the thought of being around food—or people, for that matter—made her feel like retching.

And how was she going to face *him*? The thought of seeing Clay Stevenson's face caused her jaw to tighten and her hands to go numb; rage and total helplessness coursed through her being at the same time. If only she could unleash her wrath on Clay. If only she could get back her sense of dignity and joy—two things he'd stolen, taken against her will.

But it was her own fault, wasn't it? If she hadn't worn that dress to the charity event, perhaps Clay never would have noticed her. She should have listened to her conscience and not gone. She should have refused to wear anything but her Amish clothes. She couldn't bear the thought of *Dat* and *Mamm* finding out. What would they say? They'd be ashamed for certain sure.

If only Thomas had been here. He could have saved her from this wickedness. Tommy could have—no, *would* have—sent Congressman Stevenson across the room. If Thomas knew that he'd so much as touched her, there's a good chance Clay Stevenson would barely be breathing. But because of that fact, she couldn't say anything about this to Tommy until his treatments were completed. She wasn't going to lose Thomas, no matter what. *If the treatments fail…*no, she wouldn't think about that, wouldn't even entertain the thought. Tommy was going to get well. He *had to* get well.

"Lilly?" Candace's sweet voice echoed through the door.

"*Jah?*"

"May I come in?"

"Uh, *jah.*" Lillianna quickly pulled the blanket up around her neck.

The door creaked open. Candace gasped when Lilly's cold eyes met hers. "Lilly, are you sick? What happened to your face? Your cheek looks bruised."

Lillianna began to panic. *I have a bruise?* She touched her hand to her cheek and felt the soreness.

She hadn't looked in the mirror, was too ashamed to. "I... I'm not feeling well."

"Oh my, you don't look well at all. I'll call the doctor and—"

"No! I don't want to see a doctor. I just need to rest." The last thing she desired was having to explain her condition to a physician.

Candace put her hand over Lillianna's forehead and frowned. "Well, at least there's no fever. If you get worse, I insist you see a doctor. Until then, why don't you take a couple of days off to recover? I'm capable of handling the children for a little while."

"*Denki.*"

Their eyes turned to the open door at Congressman Stevenson's voice. "What's going on?"

Lillianna quickly looked away. Clay Stevenson was the last person she desired to see or hear. As far as she was concerned, she wished she'd never have to see him again.

"Lillianna isn't feeling well. I told her to take a couple of days off," Candace said.

He frowned. "Out partying all weekend, huh? I've heard these Amish kids really live it up during their 'rump spring' or whatever it's called. Got a hangover?" He raised an eyebrow at Lillianna.

Candace gasped. "Clay, that's uncharitable."

If only Lillianna's eyes could literally shoot daggers.

"We'll let you rest now," Candace said, ushering her husband out.

Lillianna watched as the couple exited, and would have strangled her pillow to death if it had been possible.

Thomas figured Lillianna must've gone out of town with the Stevenson family, since she hadn't answered all weekend. Since it was Monday, they should have arrived back home. He picked up the phone and dialed Lil's number. One, two, three, four...he was about to hang up at the fifth ring.

"Hello?" she answered.

Thomas sighed when he finally heard Lillianna's voice. "How's the most beautiful girl in the world doing?"

"Uh, I—I haven't been feeling very well." Lillianna's voice sounded hoarse to his ears.

"Got a bad cold? You sound terrible."

"I think I'm beginning to feel better."

"I'm sorry, babe. Wish I could be there to hold you and nurse you back to health." He frowned.

"No, Tommy. You stay there and get better."

"Don't worry, Lil. I think I *am* getting better. I know I feel better."

"That's *gut*."

He didn't want to hang up, but felt he should. "Well, I'll let you go so you can get some rest."

"*Denki*." Lillianna hesitated. Did she not want to hang up either? "Tommy?"

"Yes?"

"Have you watched any of the videos yet?"

He knew it was coming eventually. "I have."

"And?"

"They're quite compelling. I'll be honest with you. That man has seriously challenged some of the things I believe. I want to do some research to see if what this guy is saying is true."

"I'm glad."

"Don't hold your breath, Lil."

"I won't. I'll pray. That's much more effective."

Thomas chuckled. "That's one of the things I love about you. Ever faithful."

"Well, I better go now." Lillianna never did know how to receive praise.

"I love you, Lil."

"I love you too, Tommy. Goodbye."

Chapter Twenty-Two

"Lillianna, Clay and I have been talking," Candace said, over their morning cup of coffee. "We purchased an extra ticket and we'd like you to come on the cruise with us so we can have more time for social engagements."

Lillianna nodded. She wasn't thrilled with the idea, but at least she wouldn't have to worry about Congressman Stevenson staying back to "finish up work".

"You'll need some other clothes, so we'll have to go shopping. Don't worry. We'll be paying for your outfits."

"My Amish clothes are not good enough?"

"I'm afraid not. It would probably be best for Clay and for you if people didn't know you're Amish. It would bring too much publicity and we'd rather stay away from that, especially after that last article they printed."

Lillianna nodded slowly.

"Don't worry. We'll find you some modest out-fits." Candace glanced up at the clock. "We don't have much going on this evening. Let's go today after Clay gets home. He can watch the children so we can shop worry-free."

"He will watch the *kinner*?"

Candace laughed. "He does that once in a while to give me a little time to myself. He's pretty good with them."

"If you think that would be okay." Lillianna couldn't imagine leaving her own children with that man, but these were *his* children. Perhaps she shouldn't be concerned. Just knowing what he was capable of, though, cast doubt on his character. Clay Stevenson was nothing like the man those around him perceived him to be. "We could take them with us."

Candace smiled and shook her head. "You've never seen them at the mall."

You've never seen your husband alone with me. Lillianna wished with all her heart that she could utter those words, but she didn't have that liberty. She would keep her secret for as long as she had to—just until Thomas finished his treatments.

Upon receiving his mail, Thomas retreated to his room for privacy. He pulled out the envelope he'd been anticipating—a letter from his sister. He ran his hand over his sister's handwriting and a wash of memories swept over him. He remembered harvesting tobacco with *Dat* and his two younger brothers, Eli and William. Most of the women were inside working, but his sister, Rhoda, had been penning a letter to her beau, who eventually became her husband. Those were some of the happiest times in his life; well, along with meeting his sweet girl at the pond.

Thomas shook his head to refocus. They'd be serving dinner soon, so he only had a few minutes of quiet time. A lump stuck in his throat as he slipped his finger under the envelope flap. What would Rhoda say? Would she chastise him for leaving their siblings behind?

Dear Thomas,

Greetings in the name of our Lord!

You don't know what good it did my heart when I received your letter! The truth is I'd been frettin' about you, wondering if you were still alive. I'm very sorry to hear that you have cancer. I will pray for you.

You didn't say in your letter if you are still Amish or no. I hope you are. You know that Bishop Mast will require a kneeling confession if you're to come back home. I will not be able to allow you into our home. I'm sorry, but you know that is the way it has to be. We can still visit outside, jah?

If you want to join a faster district nearby, I 'spect Bishop Hostettler will probably re-

ceive you. You know they are not as strict to the Old Ways. I'm certain sure Bishop Mast wouldn't like me suggesting that to you, but I'd rather have you near than somewhere far away. Mamm *and* Dat *would probably want you close too.*

Our brieder *and* schweschdern *are well. Katie got herself hitched last fall to Ira Yoder. They're expectin' a* boppli *now. The boys are growin' big and you have yet to meet your niece and nephew. I miss you, Thomas. I hope you'll come back home.*
Only your sister,
Rhoda

Thomas folded the letter and slid it back into its envelope. It was a shame his siblings were still so steeped in tradition. A visit would be difficult, no doubt, but it didn't negate his desire to see them. Of course, a visit would still be many months off, if not over a year.

He desired to take Lillianna on a nice honeymoon. Hawaii, perhaps?

Candace and Lillianna walked through the ladies' section of the department store. Other than in Candace's closet and *Mamm's* garden, Lillianna had never seen such an array of colors. She'd certainly never had this many hues to choose from. Most of

them had been forbidden her entire life. She'd been
restricted to blues, grays, and browns mostly.

"Choose several tops and bottoms, then you can
try them on," Candace urged.

Lillianna browsed through several racks of clothing, but had a difficult time deciding what would be
appropriate. "Where are the dresses?"

"Dresses?" Candace smiled. "They would be in
a different section. You may select some skirts and
tops as well, if you prefer them to pants." She led
the way to another section of the ladies' department.

"I don't know what to choose," Lillianna admitted.

"Would you like for me to give you suggestions?"
Lillianna nodded.

"Personally, I love to mix and match."

Lillianna's lips twisted. She had no idea what
Candace was talking about.

"See? Take this floral skirt and find two tops that
will go with it—tops that are the same color as some
of the flowers or leaves in the skirt. You could get a
plum-colored shirt and also a green one. Both would
look great with this. If you buy plain skirts, you can
do the same thing."

Lillianna smiled. This idea of shopping appealed
to her more and more. But she must be cautious and
not set her heart on worldly things. She was only
shopping for *Englisch* clothes because it was what
the Stevensons insisted on. She had a distinct feel-

ing, though, that Thomas wouldn't mind seeing her in some of these outfits too.

"When we're done here, we'll have to go find you a bathing suit."

"Bathing suit? I don't think I'd be comfortable wearing an *Englisch* bathing suit." Lillianna had to speak up. She couldn't imagine being half-dressed in a public place, especially if Clay Stevenson was anywhere around.

"Don't worry, Lilly. They do have modest bathing suits, and we can buy a cover-up if you'd like. That's like a small dress that goes over the suit."

Lillianna blew out a breath. This was definitely out of her comfort zone.

"You'll need a bathing suit to take the children to the pool."

"There's a pool on the boat?" Lillianna's eyes bulged.

Candace nodded. "Just wait, Lilly. You're going to have the time of your life."

Somehow, Lillianna couldn't imagine *ever* having a good time so long as Clay Stevenson was around.

Chapter Twenty-Three

"Well, I'd say you're lucky," Thomas' voice echoed through the telephone.

Lillianna's chin dropped. "Lucky?"

"Yeah. Think about it, Lil. You live in a fancy house with everything you can imagine at your disposal. You get to ride around in a limousine; most people pay hundreds of dollars to rent those for just a few hours. Now, you're going on a luxury cruise and you don't have to pay a penny."

Thomas had no idea. What he saw as a dream-come-true, was actually a nightmare.

"The Stevensons wanted me to get some *Englisch* clothes for the trip—even a bathing suit. I went shopping with Candace the other day."

"A bathing suit? I'd love to see you in one of those. Uh, after we're married, of course."

"I wish you could go with me, Tommy."

"You don't know how much I'd love to. Maybe someday the two of us can go," he offered.

"I probably won't call you for a week."

"When do you leave?"

"Tomorrow. Tommy, will you…pray for me?" She had to enlist the prayers of somebody. She felt her own weren't reaching past the ceiling.

"Pray? Lil, you know I don't pray. Listen, there's no need to be nervous. You'll be fine, baby."

Tears pricked her eyes. Thomas didn't understand. It had nothing to do with anxiety. No, sheer terror could only describe her emotional state at present.

Lillianna was surprised by how much she enjoyed traveling by airplane. Perhaps being around a crowd of people brought a sense of comfort. It had been her first time in the friendly skies, since air travel was *verboten*, except in extreme circumstances like Carolanne's. Her heart ached for her friend's companionship. If she'd still been alive and healthy, surely Lillianna would have shared her woes. What advice would Carolanne have given?

Candace had become a friend, but she could only share certain things with her perpetrator's wife. She had been able to confide in Candace about Thomas and her home life, and for that she felt grateful. But she couldn't see herself *ever* telling Candace about what Clay had done. To do so would not only force Thomas out of receiving his treatments, but it would also tear a family apart.

Sometimes the right path to take is not always illuminated with bright lights. Oftentimes the path is

shrouded with a heavy fog. And sometimes sacrific-
ing for others meant persecution, abuse, and bodily
harm. Lillianna thought of Jesus and the suffering
He'd gone through on the cross. Suddenly, her situation didn't seem so bad. She would take Jesus' hand
and let Him lead her through this; it was the only way
she could possibly see her way out of the darkness.

When Lillianna discovered she'd have her own
room on the cruise ship, a burden lifted. Of course,
the room would be right next door to the Stevenson
family's. She didn't relish being that close to Clay.
In fact, if she never saw him again it would be a
dream come true.

The sheer vastness of the ship was a shock to Lillianna. She had had no idea how large cruise ships
were and she guessed Noah's Ark to have been of
similar size.

"What are those smaller boats for?" She pointed
to several rescue boats on the upper decks.

"Those are lifeboats," Clay explained. "If the ship
starts to sink, that will be how we escape. Ever heard
of the *Titanic*?"

Lillianna shook her head.

"It was a large luxury cruise ship like this one.
It hit an iceberg and began filling with water. They
didn't have enough lifeboats for everyone to escape,
so a lot of passengers drowned in the sea." He rubbed
his chin. "Wow, I can't believe you've never heard
of the *Titanic*."

"Did you watch this on television?" Lillianna

followed as Clay and Candace led the way to their rooms.

"I think they have a news special on every time the anniversary rolls around. It sank in the early 1900s, I believe. There are many books and even a couple of movies about it."

"So there will be enough boats for us to escape?"

Clay chuckled. "It's not likely to happen, but I believe they're required by law now to have enough lifeboats to rescue the passengers if need be."

"Here we are," Candace informed her.

Lillianna peeked into her room while the Stevenson family entered theirs. She hadn't known what to expect, but it was quite a bit smaller than what she'd envisioned. Nonetheless, it was pleasant and sufficient for her needs. She especially enjoyed the unique touches the crew had created for her, like the towel shaped like a swan and the candy on her pillow.

Candace had said that Lillianna would be caring for the children for a good portion of the cruise. She handed her a list of activities for children and their dates and times. The children usually took a nap after lunch, so she'd have to stay in the cabin while they napped.

"You can choose which activities to take them to, but they will especially enjoy the game room and the bowling alley. They'll love the water park too, just make sure you are with them the whole time. Only take them to the small kiddie pool where they can walk around, not the larger pool with the older children. And be sure to take them to the arts and crafts class," Candace said. "If they seem tired or start getting cranky, bring them back to the cabin."

Lillianna nodded, attempting to remember everything Candace had suggested.

"And whatever you do, don't let them out of your sight and don't let them run around on the ship. I'll explain all the rules to them and tell them that you're in charge, but you'll probably have to remind them from time to time."

"When would you like for me to watch them?" Lillianna eyed her bed, thinking a nap sounded great.

"Feel free to relax for the time being. Clay and I want to tour the ship with the children and make sure everything is safe and sanitary in the play areas. We'll probably be quite a while and we plan to nap when we return. Or you're welcome to come with us, if you'd like."

"No, thank you. I think I'll rest for a while."

The children were bursting with energy after their craft-time activity and Lillianna debated on whether it would be a good idea to allow them to attend the cupcake-decorating class. A rush of sugar was the last thing they needed. Would Candace be disappointed if she didn't take them? She'd mentioned the class earlier and raved about how much the children would enjoy it. Lillianna sucked in a breath and decided she probably should take them if their mother wanted them to go.

This evening, Candace informed her that the children would be retiring early because she and Clay had in mind to attend a special dinner. Apparently, they'd run into friends who they hadn't seen in a while so they planned to spend time with them. That was quite all right with Lillianna. This cruise ship provided too much activity for her taste.

At least the food provided had been delicious. Lillianna continued to be amazed at the extravagance. It seemed everything was an art—even the food. Some of the fruit and vegetables took the form of animals or flowers. A giant block of ice had been carved into a dolphin sculpture. There was food enough to eat as much as you wanted and it didn't surprise her that many of the guests were overly plump. Fortunately, though, many of the food choices were nutritious.

"Clay and I will be leaving shortly to meet our dinner guests. Feel free to let the children watch a movie, and then they can go to bed. We'll be out late," Candace informed her.

"Okay."

"I can bring something back for you. Something to drink—tea, water, or juice?"

Lillianna smiled. Candace was always so thoughtful. "I would like some juice."

"Is that it? I can bring some snacks too," Candace offered.

"That sounds *gut*."

"All right. I'll be back in just a little bit."

Lillianna watched as Clay and Candace made

their way in the direction of one of the dining areas.
It looked like this evening would be a pleasant one.
Tomorrow would be their last. She did as Candace
suggested and put a children's movie on for Calvin
and Camille. The children had been well-behaved
most of the time, for which she was thankful.

Chapter Twenty-Four

A knock on the door reminded Lillianna about her request for a drink and a snack. Candace must've brought them already. She pulled open the door.

"Clay?" She frowned. Not who she desired to see on her doorstep.

"Candace was busy talking so she sent me with your drink," he said. "Here's your O.J."

Apparently, he'd forgotten the snack.

She took the drink from his hand, nodded, and abruptly shut the door. No need to give Clay any ideas.

Lillianna overheard Clay talking to the children in the room next door. There was a door between the two rooms so one could be easily accessed from another. Candace had said it would be fine to leave the children to watch the movie so long as she kept their main door locked and she could hear them. Until she heard Clay, she'd left the door open. She'd leave it closed until she was certain he'd gone.

Several moments later, she could only hear the children's movie. She opened the door to peek in and see if Clay had gone. Fortunately, he had. Lillianna yawned, beginning to feel drowsy. She glanced at the alarm clock near her bed, but the numbers were blurred. Why did she feel this way?

Another knock on the door informed her she should answer. She slothfully moved toward the door and pulled it open.

Clay had returned.

Lillianna awoke with a massive headache. She attempted to sit up, but her body seemed to ache all over. What was going on? Was she coming down with the flu?

"Lilly, are you okay?" Candace leaned over her bed.

She could barely catch her breath. "I… I think so."

"Do you need to stay here and rest a while longer? Clay and the children and I are going to the theater to watch a show. Do you want us to go without you?"

Lillianna nodded.

After the Stevensons left, she attempted to go back to sleep but she couldn't. Other than feeling lousy, she had difficulty recalling the events of the night before. As a matter of fact, she couldn't remember going to bed. She rubbed her temples attempting to bring back some sort of recollection. The last thing she remembered was… *Clay.* He'd brought her juice.

The door adjoining the two rooms swung open and Clay stood in the midst.

"Are you okay?" He seemed concerned.

"You did something, didn't you?"

Clay smirked. "I'll never tell." He came and sat at the edge of her bed.

She poked a finger in his chest. "You...you put something in my drink."

"Think what you want." He shrugged.

"I *know* you did," Lillianna insisted.

"Trust me, baby, you enjoyed it as much as I did. Every minute of it." He reached out to touch her cheek, but she quickly turned away.

"I don't know how you sleep at night," she said in disgust.

"Rather well, actually. Of course, if you'd join me *willingly* I think I could sleep even better." He raised his eyebrows twice in quick succession. "What do you say just the two of us get away for a few days? Wherever you want to go."

"Never."

"We'll see about that." He opened the door to exit her room. "We can discuss this later. My wife and kids are waiting for me in the auditorium. Think on my proposal."

If Lillianna's head didn't ache so much, she'd want to roll around on the floor, kick her feet, and scream. She knew a tantrum wouldn't help her situation, but it sure would make her feel better. Would this nightmare never end?

* * *

Upon arriving home from their cruise, Lillianna discovered she'd received a letter from her sister and her mother. She opened *Mamm's* first. *Mamm* had shared news of their Amish community and spoke of how much she missed Lillianna and wished she'd return home. She also said that she understood why Lillianna was doing what she was doing, but she didn't approve of it. Despite that fact, Lillianna was surprised at the mostly positive message. She knew *Mamm* cared and desired for her to come home. Lillianna was feeling more than a little homesick herself.

Mandy's letter had been quite different. It was short—just a couple of sentences.

> *Dear Lilly,*
> *I don't know if you've heard the news yet or not. Samuel Beachy died yesterday in a buggy accident. His funeral is in a couple of days.*
> Thought you'd want to know.
> *Your sister,*
> *Amanda*
> *P.S. I bet Carolanne is happy.*

Lillianna set the note down and sank into her bed. It seemed unreal that Samuel was actually gone. She'd just seen him a few weeks ago. Apparently, it hadn't been God's will for the two of them to marry. If Lillianna was honest with herself, she'd admit that having Samuel Beachy as a backup plan had given her a sense of comfort.

What would happen now if Tommy died? To the *Englisch*, it was not such a big deal to be Lillianna's age and unmarried. But to the Amish, having a husband and a houseful of *kinner* meant you'd found favor with *Der Herr*. And at her age, she was considered an old maid.

Lillianna walked to the closet and removed the quilt that Samuel had given her. She held it close to her bosom and inhaled the familiar scent, whispering a brief prayer for his family. She was reminded once again just how fragile life was. One day you could be talking with someone, and the next day they would be gone. Death was difficult to grasp, but it was a fate that we all must meet someday. Carolanne and Samuel had been ready and she felt she was too, but what of Thomas? *Nee*, she didn't think Thomas was ready for eternity.

Chapter Twenty-Five

Lillianna brought a shaky hand to her mouth. She stared down at the pregnancy test again and tears pricked her eyes. It was bound to happen sooner or later. *No! Why, God? I don't understand why You would allow this to happen. What am I going to do? How am I going to tell Thomas?*

A light knock sounded on the door and Lillianna quickly set the pregnancy test inside the drawer. "Coming!" she called from the bathroom.

She pulled the bedroom door open and frowned at Clay Stevenson. What did he want?

"My family is going out of town again this weekend." He smirked. "I thought you'd want to know so you can be prepared. Oh, and I bought a little something I'd like you to wear," he spoke in low tones, and reached to caress her neck.

Lillianna cringed and stepped back from his touch. Was there no end to this man's depravity? "I won't wear it. You know I won't," she protested. *Oh,*

Thomas, I wish you'd come back soon. When would she wake up from this nightmare?

"We'll see. I love it when you play hard-to-get." He caressed her cheek and she hastily turned away. The congressman chuckled, then turned to go.

"Wait!" Lillianna called.

Clay turned around and raised his eyebrows.

"I'm pregnant," she blurted out.

He mumbled a curse under his breath. Clay stepped into her room and closed the door behind him. He spoke calmly, "I'll take care of it. I know a doctor. I'll take you in first thing next week."

"A doctor? I said I'm pregnant, I don't need to see a doctor." She'd known many Amish women who'd never once seen a doctor their entire pregnancy. A doctor was only necessary if there were complications.

"He'll get rid of it for us." Clay looked at her pointedly. "You're getting an abortion."

She shook her head adamantly. "No, I won't do it. Never. You can't make me. I won't do it!"

"Calm down before my wife and kids hear you," he hissed. He turned back to the door. "On second thought, maybe we should wait a while longer so this doesn't happen again."

Lillianna frowned.

"We'll discuss this later." He pulled the door open to exit and his wife stood in front of him.

"Oh, did I interrupt something?" Candace asked.

Lillianna bit her lip.

Clay bent down and kissed his wife on the lips. "No, honey. I was just informing Lilly here that we are going out of town again this weekend. I closed the door because I didn't want to wake the children." He raised his eyebrows and winked at his wife. "I can't wait."

Lillianna felt like rolling her eyes. *How can this man be so double-minded? Does Candace actually believe his words?*

Candace smiled. "I'm so glad I married you."

Apparently so.

"And I, you." Clay slowly kissed her lips again. He raised his eyebrows and cocked his head toward their bedroom. Candace smiled and nodded.

Lillianna looked away in disgust.

Clay stepped out of the room and pulled the door closed. It opened again within a split second. "Oh, Lilly. I forgot to tell you that Thomas called. He'd like for you to call him back this evening," Candace said, and handed her the cordless phone. Lillianna realized she must've left it downstairs again.

Lillianna nodded and set the phone down on her nightstand. "Thank you. I will call him."

She shut the door and clenched her fists tightly. *Ugh, Clay's such a jerk!* Lillianna felt bile rising in her throat and ran to the bathroom. This pregnancy wasn't going to be easy by any stretch of the word.

Lillianna stared at the phone in her hand. She'd been in the same position for ten minutes now. What would she say to Thomas? And how? She'd previously decided to not even mention the rape, but now she had no choice but to tell him. *God, please help me.*

As she slowly dialed the number, her hands trembled.

"Hey, sweetie!" Thomas' voice on the line was so soothing. She'd give anything to have him home and healthy.

"Hi." She couldn't manage much more. Several seconds passed.

"You're quiet tonight. Need to talk about something?"

She let out a sob.

"Hey, now. What's wrong, Lil? Are you crying?"

"Thomas, I… I'm…" Lillianna glanced down at her belly. She thought of Clay's words about cutting off the money for Tommy's treatment.

"You're what?"

"I—I just miss you so much, Tommy." She held back another sob.

"I miss you too, baby. I can't wait to get home and marry you. You know I love you, don't you?"

Lillianna ached to tell him the truth, but how could she? She knew if she told Thomas, he'd rush home right away, forsake his treatments—the only hope he had of becoming whole again, and rescue her. Oh, how she longed to be rescued! But not at the expense of losing Tommy. She'd go through anything to see Thomas well again, even if it meant dealing with Clay Stevenson. "I love you too. Tommy..." She sniffled. "Please come home soon."

"As soon as I can. Not a moment longer." Lillianna heard voices in the background. Thomas spoke again, "Listen, I've gotta go, Lil. Tonight's video night. It's part of the program. We've been watching health videos and I'm learning a lot. I have so much to tell you when I get home."

"Goodbye, Tommy."

Lillianna clicked the phone off and dove into her pillow. *What now, God?*

Chapter Twenty-Six

Lillianna didn't know how she was going to do it or what she would say, but Candace had to know she was expecting a baby. She wouldn't be able to hide it much longer as her dresses were already becoming too tight.

She'd tucked the children into bed nearly a half hour ago, so they were most likely sleeping. Lillianna took a deep breath and went to face Candace. Of course, Clay had already known for months.

Lillianna approached the couch where Candace sat reading a book. Clay sat on a recliner reading the paper. This arrangement seemed to be a nightly occurrence.

"I thought I needed to tell you. I'm expecting a baby," Lillianna admitted.

"A baby? You're pregnant?" Candace's mouth hung open.

"*Jah.*" She twisted her hands together in front of her abdomen.

Clay spoke up, "Who's the father?"

She looked at Clay in disbelief. He knew very well who the father was. Why would he ask such a question and in front of his wife?

"Is it Thomas?" Candace asked.

Lillianna shook her head.

"Oh, I see. So you don't even know whose baby it is." Clay looked on her with contempt.

"Clay, leave her alone."

"No, Candace. This is our home. She can't be bringing strange men over here while we're gone." Clay raised his eyebrows. "What is your Thomas going to say about this?"

Lillianna shrugged. "I don't know."

"You should get rid of it."

Candace gasped. "Clay, how could you say such a thing? That's not your decision to make."

"This is our house." He turned to his wife and gestured toward Lillianna. "If she's not going to do something about that illegitimate child, I think she needs to go. We can't have her setting a bad example for our children, Candace."

"But, the money…"

He thrust two fingers in her direction. "You should have thought of that before you hopped into bed with…"—he threw his hands up—"…who knows who. Do you *honestly* think Thomas will still want you when he finds out that you've been sleeping around?"

Of all the nerve! Lillianna wanted to scream. How

could this wretched man say such things when *he* was the one to blame? Her eyes filled with tears.

"Clay, I think we need to discuss this before we make any hasty decisions," his wife attempted to reason. She looked at Lillianna sympathetically. "We... we can adopt the child."

"We'll do no such thing!" Clay insisted.

The last thing Lillianna desired was to leave this baby in Clay's home.

"You'll give the baby up for adoption, then," Clay stated matter-of-factly.

"Clay, that's her decision to make, not ours," Candace gently reminded. She turned to Lillianna. "Thank you for letting us know."

Lillianna nodded, then hurried back up to her room where she could pour her heart out to God once again.

"If you're going to insist on having this baby, I insist that you put it up for adoption," Clay demanded.

"Why?" Lillianna frowned and rubbed her expanding belly.

"I can't believe you're asking me why. You're much smarter than that, Lilly. You know as well as I do that if you keep that baby, people will ask questions."

"I won't lie."

Clay laughed out loud. "You won't have to if you give the baby away. I can find a good family for it."

"What if I want to keep it?"

"No."

"You can't make me give it away."

"Yes, I can." His eyes warned.

"If you do, I'll tell Candace."

"She'd never believe you over me. And if she does, I'll tell her you seduced me."

"I'm keeping the baby."

Clay threw up his hands in defeat. There was no sense in arguing with a senseless woman. Besides, he had in mind to put the baby up for adoption anyway. "Okay. You keep the child if you want; I will have nothing to do with it. But I promise you this, Lillianna. If you *ever* tell anyone the truth of what happened between us, I will see to it that the baby doesn't survive. It doesn't matter where you are. I swear, I will find you and you will never see that child again."

She stared back into Clay's stone-cold eyes. Oh, how she loathed this wicked man.

"Do I make myself clear?"

Lillianna quickly looked away, but he grasped her chin and forced her to look at him again.

"I said, do I make myself clear?"

Lillianna briefly nodded.

"Good. We have an understanding." Clay scratched his head. "You know, you'd be wise to reconsider." His eyes pierced hers one last time before he trudged out the door.

Chapter Twenty-Seven

Thomas could scarcely believe he'd been in Mexico for ten months. They told him that some patients had a longer healing period than others, as was his case. Usually, if the patient had previously undergone chemotherapy, as he had, their healing took longer than someone whose body hadn't been damaged by the drug. If Thomas had known about this before, he could have skipped the chemo altogether and he'd have been well a long time ago. But, he surmised, the doctors couldn't tell him what they didn't know.

He took a couple of pairs of pants and packed them into his luggage bag. Boy, was he ready to see Lil! He couldn't wait to kiss her lips and tell her they could have their happily ever after now. Well, as soon as she finished working for Congressman Stevenson.

The telephone beside his bed rang and he snatched up the receiver. "Lil?"

"*Ach, nee,* Thomas. This is Rhoda," a timid female voice said.

Thomas frowned. "Rhoda? What's going on? Why are you calling me here?"

"It's Simon, he's been in an accident." His distraught sister sobbed.

"What happened?"

"His tractor tipped over and crushed his legs. Can you come home, Thomas? I need you here. It will be too much for me to have to care for Simon and the *kinner*. We have our two little ones, with another one on the way. Will you take our *brieder* and *schweschdern*?"

"What about Katie?"

"She has a new little one and is already having a time of it. I don't think Ira would like to take them in. He's not the patient type."

Thomas rubbed his forehead. "Uh… I don't know. I mean, let me call you back. I need to talk to Lillianna first."

"I will wait here at the shanty for you to call me back," Rhoda said.

"Okay."

Thomas hung up the phone and ran a hand through his hair. Life sure did present some challenges at times. What about him and Lillianna getting married? When would that take place now? The doctor had given him a clean bill of health just yesterday and said his treatments were complete. As long as he kept eating as they'd prescribed, his cancer should not return.

Lillianna still had a couple of months left to work

for the congressman, so she would not be able to leave yet.

Thomas dialed Lillianna's phone number and listened to it ring about ten times. *Not now!* It looked like he'd have to make this decision on his own. He dialed Rhoda's phone number and she quickly picked up.

"Okay, it'll take me about a week, but I'll be there. I'm going to swing by where Lillianna is working, then I'll come right away," he informed his sister.

"*Gut*, Thomas. *Denki*."

Lillianna wiped the sweat from her brow and took two quick, labored breaths.

"That's right, Lilly. You can do this," Candace coaxed.

She glanced up at the doctor again, hating the fact that he was watching this whole process. Lillianna would've much more preferred their Amish midwife. It still would've been awkward, but at least she was female.

Another labor pain seized her abdomen, stealing her breath away. When would this be over? A hundred thoughts swirled in her head, but her main concern was giving this *boppli* up to someone else. A stranger. Giving a child away went against everything she'd ever been taught and believed. Conceived in rape or not, she didn't know if she could do it. Yet, Clay had said the adoptive parents would be coming for the baby tomorrow. They would have been here sooner, had they known she'd go into labor four weeks early. But who could predict these things? How did she let him talk her into this?

Oh no! "I… I need to go to the bathroom." Lillianna looked up at Candace with pleading eyes. If she didn't go right now, she'd be in trouble.

"That's the baby coming," Candace assured. "Do you feel like you need to push?"

Lillianna nodded desperately.

"Go ahead. Anytime you're ready," the doctor said.

Lillianna grasped the sheet that covered her body, leaned forward, and pushed with all her might. She fell back on her pillow exhausted.

"That's all right, you're doing great," Candace said, stroking her arm.

Lillianna pushed for ten more minutes. She didn't know if she had the stamina to do this anymore.

"Come on, you're almost there. I see the head crowning," the doctor urged.

She nodded at the doctor, then looked to Candace, thankful this kind woman was at her side.

"You can do it, Lillianna. Trust me, I've done it twice." Candace smiled, offering reassurance.

Lillianna had gained a new appreciation for the many Amish women she knew with ten and twelve children. How did they do this so many times?

A few moments later, Lillianna watched as the doctor held a tiny dark-haired baby girl. The baby let out a healthy cry and Lillianna's heart ached. How could she give this precious little one to a complete stranger? The nurses took the baby and cleaned her up, then put her into a plexiglass cradle to be wheeled off to the nursery.

"Wait! Please, let me hold her," Lillianna begged.

The nurse shrugged and brought the baby to Lillianna. She was sure if Clay or Candace hadn't left, that they'd insist on her not seeing or holding the baby. But she *had* to. She couldn't give the baby up without at least gazing upon her once. The nurse left, giving her the privacy she desired.

Lillianna examined every precious inch of this sweet infant. She wished she could name her. A tear slipped down her cheek as reality set in.

Help me, God. My heart is torn. As I gaze upon this beautiful angel in my arms, my emotions are all ferhoodled. *I desire with all my heart and soul to keep this precious one. I want to love her all of my days. I long to hold her tight when she's afraid, to nurse her back to health when she is sick, to kiss away the pain when she is hurt. But I'll never be able to do any of those things. I know I will forever live with the regret of this moment. Help me through this. Please, help us both.*

The baby became restless and began to suck on her fingers. She let out a wail and Lillianna instinctively put the baby to her breast. She gently fingered the baby's fine hair and placed a kiss on her forehead. This felt so natural, so right.

"What are you doing?" Clay stomped in.

"She's hungry."

Clay snatched the baby up. "No. You can't do this. You're putting her up for adoption."

Lillianna shook her head. "I don't want to. I want to keep her."

"Don't be ridiculous. You're not keeping her." The baby cried, but Clay didn't attempt to calm her.

Lillianna reached for the baby, but he refused to give the baby to her. "Why not? I'm her mother. I can raise her better than anyone can. I love her."

"Oh, really? And tell me how you plan to support her."

"Thomas and I are getting married."

Clay roared with a sarcastic chuckle. "You are living in a fairy-tale world. Do you really believe Thomas is going to raise another man's baby? Wake up, Lillianna. *No* man would ever do that."

Tears filled Lillianna's eyes. What if Clay's words were true?

Chapter Twenty-Eight

Thomas couldn't tamper the spring in his step or the thrill in his heart. His pulse quickened with every step he took, knowing he'd be seeing his soon-to-be wife within seconds. As much as he'd wanted to see her the moment he'd returned, he forced himself to stop at Tyrone's to take a shower and shave. He'd rented a car in San Diego and drove practically nonstop.

He called the landlord for a rental property in Pennsylvania yesterday to be sure their home would be available. Now that he was cancer-free and feeling better than he had as a teenager, he had plenty of strength and energy to begin working again. By his calculations, they would have enough money saved up within two years' time to put a decent down payment on their own home. And by then, they'd hopefully have a little one on the way. He was certain Lillianna wouldn't mind that he'd agreed to care for his siblings. Besides, it was more than likely to be only temporary.

Thomas made his way up the magnificent drive, located on the east side of the home. Each of the two driveways was decorated with an ornate fountain and ornamental topiaries. He stood for a second and marveled at the congressman's fancy house, amazed that his fiancée had the privilege of working in such an estate. No doubt Lillianna had gotten spoiled living in the lap of luxury for nearly a year. Feelings of insecurity and inadequacy surged in his gut. Hopefully she wouldn't be disappointed with the little cottage Thomas had chosen as their temporary dwelling place.

He pushed the button for the doorbell and waited for what seemed like centuries. In reality, it was less than a minute.

"Tommy?" Lillianna's eyes widened.

Boy, was she a sight for sore eyes. "I'm done, Lil. I'm whole."

"That…that's great!" Had Lil hesitated before embracing him? She didn't exactly portray the excitement *he* was feeling. It seemed…forced.

Thomas pulled Lillianna close and breathed in the scent of her hair. Oh, it felt so good to hold her in his arms again. He moved to give her the kiss he'd been dreaming about since he'd left. She allowed a brief kiss, then quickly turned her cheek, to his disappointment. Perhaps she didn't feel this was the proper place.

"Where's everybody at?"

"Uh, Candace took the children to the park. I think Clay is in his office."

Why did Lil seem nervous? She certainly wasn't acting normal.

"Did I hear a baby?" His eyes brightened and he looked past her.

A momentary frown flashed across Lillianna's face. "Uh...*jah*. She was napping."

"I didn't even know Clay's wife was expecting. May I see the baby?"

Lillianna nodded.

Thomas followed as Lillianna led the way to a bedroom. They climbed the carpeted spiral staircase, holding onto the thick mahogany rail. "Wow, this place is nicer than I'd realized."

Lillianna remained quiet.

Thomas couldn't shake the uneasy feeling he was experiencing. It was almost as though he and Lil were strangers. No mind, they simply needed more time together to get reacquainted and rekindle their mutual passion for one another.

When Lillianna opened the bedroom door, the baby began crying more. She rushed to the little one and swept her up into her arms. "Shh...there now. I'm here."

"The baby sleeps in your room?" His brow rose.

She nodded.

Thomas moved close. When he saw the small bundle, he remembered the birth of his youngest siblings and joy swelled in his heart. With any luck, it wouldn't be too long before he and Lil had one of their own. "She's adorable. May I hold her?"

Lillianna handed the infant to him.

He held the baby away from his chest. "Well, let me look at you." As his eyes roamed over the little one, he marveled at how wonderful a new life was. He focused on the baby's tiny hands, feet, and face. He glanced at Lillianna, then back at the baby. He frowned. "The baby looks a little like you. That's odd." He studied the infant at length, puzzled at what his eyes beheld. She certainly did resemble Lil.

Lillianna swallowed.

"Thomas," a male voice echoed from the bedroom door. "We didn't realize you'd be back so soon."

Thomas turned to see Congressman Stevenson. "I wanted it to be a surprise for Lil."

"Lil, huh? That's cute." A look passed between the congressman and Lillianna. Did they share a secret or some sort of inside joke?

Thomas frowned. He looked back down at the baby's face. Her distinct cheekbones and jaw seemed to resemble the congressman's. *No one is home except Lillianna and the congressman. Lil is acting nervous; her countenance seems*—he glanced at Lil—*guilty?* What was going on here?

"Thomas is through with his treatments. He's all better now," Lillianna said, her voice light and airy, and obviously fake.

Thomas attempted to focus on the conversation,

but another voice seemed to drown out their words. *This baby is Lillianna's.* He handed the baby back to Lillianna.

"What's going on here, Lil?" Thomas demanded.

Lillianna laid the baby in the cradle. "What do you mean?" she whispered. Instead of making eye contact, her eyes focused on a dresser drawer.

He may have been born on a Saturday, but it wasn't last Saturday. "Don't you dare ask me what I mean! You know good and well what I'm talking about. Why does the baby look like *you*? And *him*?" His eyes pierced the congressman's. "That baby is yours, isn't it?"

Lillianna resembled a deer caught in the headlights. "Tommy, I—"

"He found us out, Lil," the congressman said with a slight smirk.

"The article was true," Thomas spat out in disgust.

Rage pumped through every vein in Thomas' circulatory system. It was only a matter of seconds before his anger ruptured and he ended a man's life. *I'm away from my girl for less than a year and she has an affair with her employer?* Thomas clenched his fist and delivered a blow to the congressman's gut, and then another to his face. He unleashed another, then another, until the man lay flat on the floor, unmoving.

Thomas walked to Lillianna, who was shaking like a leaf, and raised a clenched fist. He noticed the fear in her eyes and stopped, then lowered his hand. He couldn't do it. No matter how much she'd hurt him, he could never hurt her. His pained eyes met hers. "Thanks, Lil. Thanks for everything. You wanted me well and you got your wish. The only thing is now I wish I hadn't survived." He pressed against her and kissed her on the mouth for as long as he could stand it. His hand lingered on her ivory cheek for a moment and her breath caught. He caught the desire in her eyes—and the regret. He wished he could do more. He longed to show her the love he'd kept bottled inside—the love *he'd* saved for their wedding night in vain. "I want to remember what that felt like, and I want you to remember what you gave up." Thomas turned on his heel and walked out the door.

Lillianna's heart pounded, but her mouth couldn't find any words to speak. *What just happened?* Her breaths came in short gasps. *Thomas thinks I committed adultery with Clay.* Her whole body began trembling. She watched in silence through the window as Thomas got into his car, slammed the door, and sped away.

No! She had to explain. Even if she couldn't speak the reality of her situation, she had to say *something.* She couldn't lose Thomas.

"Come back, Thomas!" she screamed too late. Where was he going?

The baby wailed and Lillianna retrieved her from

the crib. She held the baby close to her breast, shunning the bottle of formula she was instructed to give her for nourishment. No matter what Clay dictated, she was raising this *boppli* the way she saw fit. Thomas and Clay might not want this precious one, but Lillianna loved her with all her heart.

A moan turned her attention to the congressman on the floor. Blood flowed from his mouth onto the carpeted floor. She hadn't stepped in when Thomas demonstrated his physical advantage over Clay; she only wished she could have done the same thing eight months ago. If Clay Stevenson never woke up again, she wouldn't feel sorry.

Lillianna sat on her bed, ignoring Clay on the floor, and held the baby close. This precious one was all she had now. She was bound by Clay's dictates, and because of that she'd lost Thomas. She'd sacrificed for Thomas' life, and now she sacrificed a life with Thomas for the baby's life. It all seemed so unfair.

"Why, God?" she cried silently.

I was abused and murdered so wicked mankind can have eternal life, yet they reject Me daily. Now you know how I feel when people reject My sacrifice.

Did she hear the voice or had she just imagined it?

This child is a gift. Take her and show her My love.

Finally, Lillianna understood what to do, but

where would she go? "Where should I go?" She
waited, but the answer never came. Apparently, God
must've wanted her to figure out some of this herself.

Chapter Twenty-Nine

Lillianna didn't know what to do with Clay. He'd been lying on the floor for ten minutes and she would have left him there, had she not feared Candace and the children returning. Now that the baby was sleeping soundly again, she decided that she'd better help Clay get up.

"You need to get up," she said, shaking Clay's shoulder.

He groaned.

"Hurry and get up before Candace and the *kinner* come home," she urged. "Clay, do you hear me?"

He mumbled something unintelligible.

She turned him over on his back.

"Oh," he moaned. He placed his hand over his face. "I gotta hand it to you; Thomas is a strong one." He attempted to sit up. "Help me." He reached out a hand to Lillianna.

She got behind him and tried to hoist him up. "I

really shouldn't be doing this. I'm not supposed to lift anything heavy."

"Are you implying something?" He chuckled.

How can he joke at a time like this?

He clumsily scrambled to his feet, using the bureau as a crutch, and grasped the doorframe to steady himself. "Ugh… I feel like a piece of meat that's been hammered with a tenderizer."

Lillianna couldn't help but smile. She had to admit feeling a sense of satisfaction while watching Thomas knock the daylights out of Clay.

"You'll leave now," Clay said.

"What?" Lillianna's mouth dropped.

"You heard me. It's best if you go now, before Candace and the children return."

Panic began to set in. *Leave?* She'd wanted nothing more than to leave the second she saw Clay for who he was. She'd dreamed of Tommy coming to rescue her. But now that Thomas had rejected her and she couldn't tell him the truth, she had no plans. "Now? But I still have two months. Where will I go? How will I get there?"

"Here's money." He dug into his wallet and handed her a wad of cash. "Jones will take you where you want to go. I don't ever want to see you back here again."

"But what about the baby? How will I have money to raise her? To buy her diapers?"

"*You* wanted to keep her; figure it out. That's not

my concern." He held his head in his hands in obvious pain. "That's what welfare is for. Use it."

Lillianna frowned. Taking government handouts had always been frowned upon by her people. "I can't take someone's money for nothing. It would be wrong."

"The choice is yours." Clay shrugged then winced.

Lillianna glanced around. Where should she start?

"Make sure you take everything, even the clothes Candace bought for you and the baby. We won't have need of them here."

"I don't have room in my bag for all of it," she argued. She took Carolanne's quilt and the clothes she'd brought with her and placed them on the bed.

Clay left momentarily and returned with a rolling suitcase. "Use this."

"I can't take all this. How can I carry two suitcases, a quilt, a diaper bag, and the baby?"

"Relax. Jones will help you load up here, and unload wherever your destination is," Clay insisted. "You know, I'm going to miss you. We had a lot of fun."

Lillianna turned around and glared at him. She crossed her arms over her chest. "*You* had fun. I had no choice." She continued packing her things. "You don't need to stand there and watch me, I can handle this myself."

"You just complained about having to carry everything. I can at least carry the suitcases downstairs for you."

Lillianna rolled her eyes. "Thank you for your kindness." She watched as he picked up one of the bags off the bed and groaned. No doubt he was still in a lot of pain.

She looked around the room to make sure she hadn't forgotten anything. The baby slept soundly in the bassinet and she hated to wake her up. She sat on the bed and opened the top drawer of the nightstand. It wouldn't be *gut* if she forgot her Bible. It was the only thing that had kept her going this whole time. It seemed God always knew what she needed to hear and when she needed to hear it. She opened the beloved book one more time before she packed it away in her purse.

The words on the page jumped out at her. *But I say unto you, Love your enemies, bless them that curse you, do good to them that hate you, and pray for them which despitefully use you, and persecute you; That ye may be children of your Father which is in heaven: for he maketh his sun to rise on the evil and on the good, and sendeth rain on the just and on the unjust.* She glanced at the margin to the side of the main text and was alerted to an accompanying passage. She quickly flipped the pages. *But love ye your enemies, and lend, hoping for nothing again; and your reward shall be great, and ye shall be called children of the Highest: for he is kind unto the unthankful and to the evil. Be ye merciful, as your Father also is merciful.*

Lillianna read the passages again, this time

slowly. *I can't do it, Lord. I'm sorry.* She quickly slapped the Bible shut and shoved it into her purse. How could God ask her to not only forgive Clay, but to bless and pray for him? God may have an abundance of mercy, but she found herself lacking disparagingly. She couldn't do it.

Just ten minutes until they reached home. Many emotions churned in Lillianna's mind as she fretted about their arrival. *What would* Mamm *and* Dat *say when I arrive with a* boppli *of my own—with no father?* The thought unnerved her so much so that if she had someplace else to go, she'd ask Jones to turn around.

But there was no other place. Thomas was gone—most likely for good. Without being able to share the truth with him, she had no hope of ever reconciling with Thomas. Pain stabbed at her heart and she wiped a tear away.

The baby began to stir and Lillianna smiled as the babe stuck her bottom out and stretched her tiny arms wide. How could someone so beautiful come from such a wretched, sinful act? It had to be God's mercy; that was the only thing she could think of. *Mercy.* Yes, that is what she would name her.

"Hello, Mercy. Do you like your name?" Lillianna took the baby into her arms as the limo rolled to a stop, and braced herself for her parents' reaction.

Chapter Thirty

Thomas stared up at the sky, a forlorn look in his eye. As he walked the farmland on his sister's property, he raised his fist to the heavens. "See? This is exactly why I refuse to believe in You!" He kicked a mound of dirt in frustration. "Why didn't You just let me die? Why did You have to bring Lillianna back into my life? Is this some sort of cruel joke?"

"Who are you talking to?"

Thomas spun around at the sound of the male voice. An Amish man appeared near the wooded area that bordered his sister's property. *Must be a neighbor.*

"Uh…no one," Thomas answered.

The man nodded. "I see." He thrust a hand in Thomas' direction. "Jonathan Fisher."

Thomas shook the man's hand. "Thomas Girod." He pointed to the brown bottle Jonathan held. "Got another one of those? I could really use one right now."

Jonathan's brow rose. "Root beer?"

"Oh no, I thought it was—" He waved a hand in front of his face. "Never mind."

He chuckled. "*Jah*, my Susie gets upset when I drink this. She says it looks like the devil's brew."

Thomas pointed to the woods. "Do you live there?"

"Me? *Nee*. This is my father-in-law's place, Judah Hostettler."

Thomas rubbed his chin. "I've heard that name. Isn't he the bishop?"

"*Jah*."

Thomas noticed Jonathan staring at his *Englisch* clothes.

"Are ya thinkin' on buying this land?" Jonathan asked.

"Oh, no. This is my sister's place. She and her husband live here with their two *kinner*. He was injured pretty badly when a tractor crushed his legs. I came to help out until he recovers."

Jonathan nodded. "Would you like to come for supper?"

Thomas shook his head. "I don't think so. It's my first day back and I'm sure my sister will want me to eat with her family."

"Another time, then?"

"Uh, yeah, sure."

"So, you used to be Amish?"

"Yes. I left almost four years ago."

"Why?"

Thomas scratched his head and grimaced. "Well, both of my folks died. I guess I had a lot of questions that I needed answered."

"How did your folks die?"

"Flash flood. They were crossing a familiar stream, one we'd cross all the time. I reckon *Dat* didn't realize how much it had risen after the storm."

"I've heard those can be dangerous. I guess the water is pretty swift once it gets going. My neighbor lost a cow one time. I was down by the creek to see what had become of the storm and there was his heifer floating away."

Thomas chuckled. "I bet that was a sight."

Jonathan laughed. "*Jah*, I felt bad for her, though. She probably didn't even know what was going on."

"Like my folks." Thomas sobered.

"Did you ever get your questions answered?"

"No. I have more questions now than ever."

"Like what?"

Thomas shrugged. "Why? Why did God allow my folks to die and leave their children to fend for themselves? Why did God allow me to get cancer? Why did God bring the girl of my dreams to me, only for her to have an affair with her employer and conceive a baby out of wedlock?"

"Wow. I admit those are some tough ones." Jonathan lifted his hat and glanced up at the sky. "Why do you assume God did all these things?"

"He didn't stop them from happening."

"Maybe not. Are you a robot?"

This guy must be nuts. "What? A robot? No. Not last time I checked anyway."

"Okay. Your girl. Did someone put a gun to her head and make her sleep with her employer?"

"Hey, look. I didn't ask for details. I didn't *want* the details. They had an affair. Period. I'd rather not know any more about it."

"So she *chose* to do what she did?"

Thomas nodded.

"There's your answer. It was sin. Not God."

"Yeah, well what about my folks? What sin did they commit to have a rush of water carry them away to their death?"

"Not their sin; Adam's. When mankind chose to sin, the world became cursed. Floods, disasters, these things are all a result of sin."

"But why them?"

Jonathan shrugged. "We all have to die sometime. By the way, death is also a result of sin. Man was originally intended to live forever."

"What if I told you I believe in evolution?"

"I'd say you look a lot smarter than that."

"Ouch, that wasn't nice."

"The Bible says, '*The fool hath said in his heart there is no God.*' To deny the existence of God would be to close your eyes to the beauty around you, to close your ears to the symphony of nature, to close your nostrils to the scents wafting on the breeze, to close your mouth to the delicacies of nourishment, to close your hands to the feel of luxury, to close your mind to the ability to think, and to close your heart to the only love that can penetrate the depths of the soul. For in Him all things consist, in Him we live, and move, and have our being, and without Him we cannot help but be fools. The only reason people supposedly believe in evolution is because they don't want to believe in God. Either that, or they desire to live in sin and don't want to answer for it. There is no real proof for it whatsoever."

"I know," Thomas finally admitted to himself. "I recently found that out by some online videos my ex-fiancée directed me to. They pretty much discredited all the supposed 'proof' for evolution."

Both men turned when they heard a voice calling.

"That's my brother. I better go," Thomas said.

"Why don't you come by for supper on Friday? My house is a little ways past the schoolhouse on the right. It's a white two-story with a *dawdi haus* and a sign that says Fishers' Furniture."

"I'll do that. Thanks for the chat. It was nice meeting you, Jonathan."

Jonathan nodded. "You too."

Chapter Thirty-One

It's a good thing Lillianna hadn't expected to be treated like the Prodigal Son who'd returned home, because if she had, she would have been sorely disappointed. She *had* hoped that her family wouldn't condemn her, though.

When she arrived with Mercy in her arms, her folks had been shocked, to say the least. Her younger siblings were happy to see a *boppli*, but wondered where the *boppli* had come from. They didn't really understand that one could have a baby without a father present too, unless the father had died. They'd never witnessed a circumstance like Lillianna's in their secluded Amish community.

Dat had been livid and insisted she stay in the *dawdi haus* so as not to negatively influence the other children. As she'd expected, he said he wasn't surprised she'd returned home with an infant out of wedlock, given the article in the tabloid. He apparently believed it as the Gospel Truth.

"Any time you adamantly go against the ordinances of your authority, you open yourself up to sin. You knew better than to wear the fancy *Englisch* clothes. You'd been taught better. Their ways are not our ways, Lillianna. No doubt, that's what tempted the man in the first place," her father had said.

Lillianna supposed she could understand his point of view, but it didn't make accepting it any easier. Had he known the truth, she would hope that her father would embrace her and reassure her that life would be okay again. She desired for her father to erase the deleterious image of man's primal side that Clay had ingrained into her psyche. Isn't that the essence of what every child desired—the acceptance and comfort of a loving father?

She'd already felt the bonds of self-deprecation and carried around the guilt from her choice of clothing. That in itself had been difficult to comprehend since the majority of the women present had been dressed less modestly than her. She'd asked herself many times if the outcome would have been different had she not gone to the charity gala at all. It was an answer she'd never know for certain. Even so, it is amazing how quickly others will judge when they have no idea of the actual circumstances surrounding an incident. But *Der Herr* had been gracious to give her a verse for this as well. *He that answereth a matter before he heareth it, it is folly and shame unto him.* Fortunately, she had a different picture of her Heavenly Father.

"You may come in to eat after the others are through with eating and cleaning up," *Dat* had said. "You also need to clean up after yourself and put the food away."

"I will just eat in the *dawdi haus* if it's too much trouble," she'd said, as tears pricked her eyes. How could her father be so unsympathetic?

"Very well, then," her father had said.

Mamm had spoken up at that point. "Will you be joining the church?"

Lillianna understood the meaning behind her mother's words. *Mamm* hoped that Lillianna joining the church would make *Dat* more accepting of her. "I'm unsure yet."

Her father huffed. "Well, what are you planning to do, then? Surely you're not dreaming about that man coming to marry you."

Lillianna shook her head, uncertain of which man her father referred to. "*Nee*. No man will come. Clay sent me away. And Tommy, he has gone back home."

"You act as though you are saddened by it. Why then did you go and have another man's baby? Do you expect Thomas to be pleased with what you've done? Do you expect him to raise another man's *dochder*?"

"*Nee*."

Remember what I said. I'll be watching you.

The note wasn't signed, but it clearly bore Clay's

handwriting. A shiver of fear danced up Lillianna's arm and tingled throughout her entire body. She snatched the note from her suitcase and quickly walked to the window and looked out, just to be certain Clay wasn't there. Did he think she was going to reveal his secret? How could she when the life of her precious daughter was at stake?

Lillianna walked into the small room where Mercy's nursery was. There wasn't much in the room, but she no longer thought it would be a wise idea to let the baby sleep alone. From now on, Lillianna determined to keep Mercy with her at all times. She couldn't risk losing her. She made certain the doors and windows were locked. With Clay possibly lurking, she couldn't take any chances. She had no doubt that he'd make good on his threat. He'd already shown what he was capable of.

A knock outside the door of the *dawdi haus* caused Lillianna to jump. She quickly glanced out the window and smiled when she saw her sister.

"Mandy?" Lillianna opened the door. She wondered if her sister would be allowed to enter.

Amanda looked at her new husband, James, and he nodded. "Will you wait for me at *Dat's*?" Mandy's husband smiled, gazing into her eyes an extra few seconds, then reluctantly left the two women alone.

"I missed you at meeting on Sunday," Mandy said.

"I don't know if I'll be going back." Lillianna shrugged. "I'm sure you've heard."

Amanda nodded. "Where is she?"

"She's sleeping in my room."

"May I see her?"

Lillianna consented, then led the way to her room.

"Do you mind if I hold her?" At Lilly's nod, Amanda picked the baby up when she squirmed a little bit. "Oh, she's so precious. She's tiny. How old is she?"

"Just three weeks."

"Oh my goodness, she's beautiful! She looks just like him."

"I know." Lillianna dipped her head, but not before seeing a thousand questions in her sister's eyes.

"I'm having a hard time understanding why. I mean, didn't you love Thomas? He was the whole reason you went to work for *him*. I'd think the fact that the man was married would have been enough to steer clear of any emotional or physical attraction you may have felt. Although, I must say, he is a good-looking man. I can't fault you for falling in love with him."

Lillianna shook her head. "I'd really rather not talk about Clay."

"But why? I just want to know why. You and Thomas seemed so in love."

"I do love Thomas."

"This makes no sense."

"Mandy, what's done is done. Now, please…"

"Okay, I'll change the subject. Is Thomas better now? Did his cancer go away?"

Lillianna nodded and an ache gripped her heart, remembering Thomas' last words to her. *You wanted me well and you got your wish. The only thing is now I wish I hadn't survived.*

"What is he doing now?" Amanda gently jostled the baby in her arms when she became restless.

"I think he went back home to Pennsylvania. He'd mentioned something on the phone before he showed up at Congressman Stevenson's house."

"What are you going to do now?"

"I don't really have much choice. Mercy and I need a home, so we'll stay here. I don't know how long *Dat* will allow us to stay, though, if I don't make a confession."

"Have you considered apologizing to Thomas?" Mandy's brow rose.

"Apologizing? *Nee.*"

"You don't think he'll ever take you back, do you?"

Tears sprang to Lillianna's eyes and she shook her head.

"Do you believe he really loved you?"

"*Jah.*"

"Then I think you should try to reconcile with him. You know that no Amish man is going to marry you. If Thomas loves you, then perhaps there's a chance he'll forgive you and take you back. If it's true that love can conquer anything, I think you have a shot. God can heal both of you. The Bible says that God is good and He's ready to forgive us; He's full of compassion, and plenteous in mercy to the ones who call upon Him. Maybe you should pray and ask God to give Thomas the mercy he needs to have toward you. Then ask Him to give you the boldness to ask for forgiveness."

There was that word again. Mercy. It was a wonderful word, indeed. But that word presented a problem. How could she expect Thomas to show her mercy for the wrong he thought she'd done, when she was unwilling to show Clay mercy for what he'd done. "I hate it when my younger sister makes more sense than I do."

"Here. I think she's hungry. She's trying to eat my shoulder." Amanda laughed.

Lillianna took the baby into her arms and planted a kiss on her plump cheek. "Mommy loves you." She nuzzled Mercy's neck, then sat down on the rocker and brought her to her breast. She looked up at her sister. "You know, life is confusing. I do regret being with Clay, but it's hard to when I have this sweet one."

"Sometimes God brings good things out of our mistakes to show us his goodness and mercy."

"I know. I don't know how I could get through all this if I didn't have little Mercy. She makes life bearable."

They both turned at a knock on the door.

"That must be James. I better go now," Mandy said.

"Thank you for coming by. You're our first visitor."

"The deacon has not come by?"

"*Nee*, not yet."

Amanda offered her a look of sympathy. "I'll come again."

"Mandy." Her sister stopped and turned to look at her. "Congratulations on your wedding. I wish I could have been there."

"*Denki*."

Lillianna stared down at the familiar passage of Scripture. "Okay, Lord. I know You want me to show him mercy and forgive him, but it's difficult. He wronged me in a big way and I'm having a hard time accepting that. I know I'm supposed to love my enemies, but how can I?"

Cast your cares upon Me.

She sucked in a deep breath. "Fine. Take it, Lord. Just take it all. I don't want to worry about this anymore. It's in Your hands now. All that I was, all that I have, all that I am and will ever be, belongs to You, God."

I will give you rest.

Lillianna closed her eyes. "Thank you, Lord."

Chapter Thirty-Two

Dear Lillianna,

I'm sorry I missed you. Clay said you had to leave quickly on an urgent matter and he let you go. I wish the children and I could have said goodbye. I'll miss you and that precious baby. Have you given her a name?

You should see poor Clay; he looks awful! He said he took a tumble down the stairs shortly after you left. I wanted him to go to the ER but he refused. You know how men are with their pride.

The children and I picked up some outfits for the baby on our shopping trip. I also bought a stroller. I went ahead and sent it along, so it should be arriving any day if it hasn't already. I hope the baby can wear the outfits. I was unsure, since you returned to your Amish community.

I also wanted to say thank you for working for us. Good help is hard to find. If you ever need another job, I'd be happy to hire you full-time.

I'll miss your friendship.
Sincerely,
Candace
P.S. I've enclosed pictures that the children drew
for you.

Lillianna looked down at the drawings from
Calvin and Camille. One showed Cammie sitting
on Lilly's lap with a book, and the other portrayed
Lilly pushing Cal on the swing. She held the precious memories to her chest. She'd become such a
part of their lives in the ten months she was in their
home that they felt like family. In a way, they were.
It was a shame that Mercy would never know her
half-brother and sister.

She opened the package accompanying the letter and found several outfits for the baby. Since she
wasn't part of the Amish church, she saw no reason
why Mercy couldn't wear the new apparel. However,
if she visited her folks, she would be certain to dress
her in Amish clothing so as not to offend them.

Thomas had been in the field all day, and quite
frankly, he was tired of staring at the back end of
a team of draft horses. A farmer's life might have
been suitable for his brother-in-law, but Thomas preferred to work with his hands. He couldn't see himself doing this for the rest of his life. Besides, just
sitting gave him too much time to contemplate the
situation with Lillianna.

He'd tried to force her memory out of his mind, but she kept reappearing over and over again. The whole situation just didn't make sense. Either that, or he didn't want it to. He wanted to believe that Lillianna was the sweet innocent girl he'd fallen in love with. After his cancer had been cured, he thought their lives would be perfect. How wrong he was! Nevertheless, he couldn't imagine never seeing Lil again and just forgetting about her.

Since meeting Jonathan Fisher, Thomas had been reading his Bible—something he hadn't done in many years. After Jonathan had challenged him on several issues, Thomas realized he had no more excuses to not believe in God. He could no longer deny Him. There was no doubt God had been working on his heart.

Lillianna sat down at her desk and penned the short note with a shaky hand. She didn't know if Tommy would even open the letter, but prayed he would. She couldn't leave things undone between them. They both needed closure to their former relationship.

When she dropped the letter off at the mailbox, the postman arrived at the same time. She glanced down at the envelopes and discovered another letter from Candace. She pushed the stroller carrying Mercy, and walked back to the *dawdi haus*. She kept the sleeping baby in her stroller and wheeled her into the bedroom so she wouldn't awaken her.

Once in the small living room, she pulled Candace's letter out.

Dear Lilly,

I hardly know what to write to you. I tried to deny any inclinations I'd had about you and Clay, but the truth always comes out eventually. Clay admitted to me that the two of you had an affair and your baby is his. I can't say that I didn't already suspect this; I'd just hoped it wasn't true.

Why? Why would you choose my husband? Were you hoping to get more money than we've already given you? Is that the reason you've torn my family apart? I trusted you, Lilly. You were my friend. I thought that if I could trust anyone, it would have been you—an Amish woman with supposed morals. How wrong I was!

Clay said that you lured him into bed when the two of you were home alone. You should be ashamed of yourself! Why couldn't you have chosen someone else? Someone who didn't already have a wife and children? There are plenty of rich single men out there. Why would you steal my children's father away?

I have no words to describe how I feel about you. I know that as a Christian, I'm not supposed to hate. I know I'm supposed to love my enemies, but I can't do that. The pain in

*my heart is too great. I've considered leaving
Clay, but he's begged me not to. He said that
he never did love you; he was just overcome
by your seductive ways. You came to him in a
bathrobe? Really?*

*If I never see you again, it will be too soon.
God forgive me, but this is the way I feel.
No longer a friend,
Candace*

After reading the letter from Candace, Lillianna
wished that she could snatch Thomas' letter back
from the postman. How could Clay force enmity between her and Candace, as though what he'd done to
Lillianna hadn't been enough already? When would
this man stop destroying lives?

Thomas sucked in a breath, unsure whether he
wanted to read the letter from Lillianna. Not reading it, though, would equate to torture. He hastily
tore open the envelope.

*Dear Tommy,
I'm sorry. Please forgive me.
Lil*

Thomas immediately crumbled the letter and
threw it against the wall. *Never!*

Chapter Thirty-Three

Lillianna held Mercy in her arms while Deacon Herschberger and Minister Miller sat in her small living room. She'd known this visit was coming, so it'd been no surprise.

"The leadership has discussed your situation. Your father says you will not be baptized into the church. Is that correct?" The deacon stared at Lillianna over the top of his eyeglasses.

"*Jah.*"

"So you do not wish to remain Amish?"

Lillianna shrugged. "I don't know. I'm not ready to make a decision yet."

"Most folks join at eighteen, yet you are…"

"Twenty-four," she informed him.

"Do you refuse a kneeling confession?" The minister raised a brow.

"I do not need to confess. I am not a member." She politely reminded them of the rules of their own *Ordnung*.

"That is true. However, if you plan to stay in this home, you must make your decision within the next six weeks."

Lillianna's jaw dropped. "So, what are you saying? I either join the church or you'll force me and my baby out of my folks' home?"

"That will be their decision, but we will advise it, *jah*."

At that moment, Lillianna understood what it felt like to be a perceived enemy of the Amish church. She knew this was how many who had left were treated, but she'd never thought they'd treat her this way, especially since she had a *boppli* to care for. Would they just turn her out to fend for herself? Apparently so.

"You cannot force somebody to believe as you do; it is wrong. They must choose this life for themselves. How can you turn a young mother and baby away from their own family? How can you claim to be doing God's will?"

"And if thy right eye offend thee, pluck it out, and cast it from thee: for it is profitable for thee that one of thy members should perish, and not that thy whole body should be cast into hell."

Lillianna gasped. She'd never heard such a gross misinterpretation of Scripture in her life. "That's not what that verse means."

"Do you, a woman, claim to have a special interpretation from God?"

"*Nee*, but—"

"Good day, Lillianna. We hope you will think on our words. Consider your little one." The leaders arose and walked to the door.

So that was it. Either she joined the Amish church against her will, or she and the baby would become homeless. What a choice.

Lillianna pulled the door open. Hopefully the ministers hadn't returned with more messages of doom.

"Thomas?" She was certain her heart rate increased to a million beats per second.

"Please, Lil. Don't say another word. Just hear me out."

Lillianna nodded. Should she invite him in?

"I'm extremely upset at what you've done. I've told myself that I can't forgive you, but God won't let me do that."

"God?"

His arms crossed his chest. "I said hear me out, please."

Lillianna bit her bottom lip.

"Yes, God. I can no longer deny Him. Anyway, if you promise me that you will never, ever, ever do anything like that again, I will take your word for it. Maybe I'm a complete idiot, I don't know. All I know is that being without you is driving me crazy. If you can promise me this, I will speak of it no more. The only condition is that we must marry."

"Marry?" Her eyes widened.

He placed a finger over her lips. "Today. No questions, no protests. If you'll agree to this, nod your head."

She nodded adamantly.

"Get your things and let's go!"

Thomas hoped he was doing the right thing. There was a good chance he would later regret this decision. It certainly wouldn't be the first time he'd given in to impulse. He knew he couldn't fully forgive Lillianna without taking this step of faith. If she played him for the fool, he'd at least be better for it because he'd known her love. He was willing to risk any loss for his beloved.

He glanced at the passenger's seat, attempting to fathom his reality. Was this real or was he dreaming? Lillianna seemed distraught. Was she, too, wondering if this was all a dream? Perhaps she was contemplating his sanity. No doubt, somebody needed to.

As frightened as he was at the possible outcome of this impending marriage, his heart soared with anticipation in spite of it. He was less than sixty minutes away from fulfilling a lifelong fantasy: making Lillianna his bride.

Lillianna held a breath, afraid that if she let it out, this would all disappear or Tommy would say it was all a joke. She glanced at her sister Mandy next to her, who offered an encouraging smile. Mandy's husband, James, stood beside Thomas. She looked toward her feet to be sure Mercy was still in her car seat. All was well.

The Justice of the Peace read the vows of which they were to repeat. This was quite different from the Amish wedding she'd always dreamed of. Aside from their two witnesses, no one else from their community was present. Lillianna was ever so thankful for her younger sister and she was certain they'd be close lifelong friends.

Lillianna wasn't surprised that James had agreed to come along. It seemed he'd do whatever his wife wished. Although their parents hadn't approved of her sister's choice, Lillianna was certain she'd made the right one.

When the officiant pronounced them man and wife, Lillianna felt like pinching herself. This was all too good to be true. She'd never believed Tommy would come back, but he'd done just that. God continued to amaze her with His abundant mercy and grace.

Chapter Thirty-Four

True to his word, Thomas hadn't brought up the past. Their wedding night had been satisfying, despite Lillianna's internal apprehension. After being coerced by Clay, she was uncertain how she was supposed to feel and act. Tommy had been loving and gentle and kind, which set her mind at ease; nothing like her encounters with Clay. She hated the fact that she had someone to compare her husband to, but at least Thomas demonstrated how an honorable man should behave.

Lillianna was thrilled to be back in Lancaster County. Thomas was anxious for her to get reacquainted with his family and to meet his new friends in the neighboring district. In addition to keeping his younger siblings a few days a week, he'd been helping out on his sister's farm, and would continue for as long as he was needed. They'd given him the *dawdi haus* to occupy, but Tommy wanted a place of their own.

The situation with Tommy's family was somewhat awkward, as Lillianna and Thomas had not committed to the Amish way. She wondered if Bishop Mast or one of the ministers would pay them a visit soon. This district was even stricter than her Ohio church, but certain allowances were made when emergencies arose, such as Thomas' brother-in-law's calamity.

"What do you think about attending meeting in Bishop Hostettler's district?" Tommy asked over supper. They'd determined to stay out of his sister's household as much as possible in order to ease her burden, so meals usually included the two of them and occasionally his siblings.

"You would want to go to an Amish church?" Lillianna's brow shot up.

He shrugged. "There are some really nice folks there that I want you to meet. They have different views on things and are not as strict as Bishop Mast."

"I think Samuel Beachy, Carolanne's husband, was from there. You met them at the Grand Canyon." She frowned. "Did I tell you that he died?"

"Samuel did?"

"*Jah.* When you were in treatment. He was in a buggy accident."

"Hmm…that's too bad. I'm sorry to hear that." He scratched his head. "If I recall correctly, I think I met some Beachys. Uh… Peter was his name."

"*Ach*, I think that is Samuel's brother. *Jah*, he and his *fraa* came to visit one year."

"Small world." He shot up from his chair at the sound of Mercy's cry. "I'll get her."

Lillianna smiled. Thomas had treated Mercy as though she were his own flesh and blood. She loved to watch the two of them interact.

"Be there in a bit," he hollered from the bedroom. "She sprung a leak."

Lillianna laughed. It amazed her that he was even willing to change Mercy's diapers. She'd never seen *Dat* demonstrate that in all her growing up years; it had always been considered a woman's job.

A few moments later, the two of them emerged from the bedroom. Thomas handed the baby to Lillianna. "I do believe she is hungry."

When Lillianna brought the baby near, she immediately began searching for her source of nourishment. "You're right."

Thomas sat back down and continued eating. "So, what do you think about what I said?"

"About Amish church?"

"Yes."

She shrugged. "I wouldn't mind going."

"Good. I'd hoped you'd say that."

Lillianna shook her head in disbelief.

"What? What was that look for?" Thomas smiled.

"You. You're so different. What changed in you Thomas?" She marveled.

"I got a heart transplant."

Lillianna's brow lowered in question.

"Jonathan and the bishop led me to the Lord. The

videos you suggested that I watch; well, I watched them while I was in Mexico. As a matter of fact, that's how I spent a lot of my free time. I would watch the videos and then do my own research to see if what the guy was saying was true. I learned so much. He debunked every evolutionary myth I'd ever believed and I had no choice but to accept the truth. I'd always thought you had to commit intellectual suicide to believe the Bible, but I found the exact opposite is true. Then when I came here and met Judah Hostettler and Jonathan Fisher, they set me straight on a lot of things and answered many of my questions."

"Oh, wow." Lillianna placed the baby over her shoulder and began to pat her back.

"I can burp her," Thomas offered.

Lillianna handed Mercy to him.

"How would you feel if I adopted her?" Thomas kissed the baby's cheek.

"Is that possible?" Lillianna worried about Clay's reaction. What if he came and tried to get custody of the baby?

"Do you think Clay Stevenson would be willing to waive his parental rights? It seems to me that he doesn't want to have anything to do with her. Has he tried to contact you at all?"

Lillianna shook her head. "*Nee*. I don't think it's a good idea. I'd rather not contact him."

"I could do it."

"I think it would be better if you didn't."

"Do you not want me to be Mercy's father, Lil?"

Lillianna read the hurt in his features. "*Nee,* it's not that. You are a *gut* father to her."

"Then what is it?"

Lillianna frowned. "What if he tries to take her away? He is a politician. He has a lot of power."

"I see your point." Thomas nodded. "I have an idea. Why don't we pray on it?"

Lillianna agreed.

Dear Lilly,

Greetings in the name of the Lord! How are you, Thomas, and the baby doing? We are good. Guess what! James and I are expecting a boppli*! I can hardly believe it. I'm so excited.*

Everything is going fine at home with Mamm *and* Dat. *I think they are pleased that Thomas married you.*

I hope you are happy in Pennsylvania. Saloma said a letter came for you from Congressman Stevenson, but Dat *sent it back. It wonders me what he had to say, not that it's any of my business. It's probably better for you and Thomas and the baby if you don't have contact with him,* jah?

Well, I better go. Supper is on the stove and James will be coming home from work soon. Love from your sister,
Mandy

Lillianna scowled. The last thing she desired was correspondence from Clay Stevenson. What did he want? She hoped that he would never find her here.

Chapter Thirty-Five

If Thomas was honest with himself, he'd admit that he was worried. Ever since he mentioned adopting little Mercy, Lillianna had seemed different. Perhaps he shouldn't have mentioned Clay Stevenson's name. Had it brought back memories for Lil? Was she still thinking of her former lover? He forced the posthole digger into the ground in frustration.

Didn't Mercy deserve a proper father? He loved that baby with all his heart. He wished she belonged to him and Lillianna.

He sighed when he looked down the row of fence posts. He'd hoped to be finished with this by noon, but it didn't look like it would happen. Dinner would be ready soon and Lil would be expecting him to come in from the field.

After setting a few more posts, he glanced up at the sun and determined by its position that it was around noon. He set the posthole tool down and began heading to the house to wash up.

A black sports car caught his eye as he neared the house. He'd seen it before. If he didn't know any better, he'd say it belonged to Clay Stevenson. He'd better be wrong. The closer he moved toward the house, the more his blood started to boil. That man had no business entering the place where he and his wife dwelt. If he knew what was good for him, he'd stay far away.

Instead of charging in, he attempted to gather his wits about him. He inched toward an open window, hoping to hear the conversation taking place inside.

"What are you doing here, Clay?" Lillianna did not sound happy to see him. That was a good sign.

"You know why I'm here. I'm taking the baby."

Oh, no.

"No. You can't. I won't let you."

"Since when do *you* have power over *me*, Lillianna? I warned you that if you *ever* told anybody about the circumstances of her conception, that I was going to get rid of that child. And I aim to do just that."

"I didn't tell anyone that you raped me! I haven't said anything to anybody."

Raped? Thomas' jaw clenched. He felt like he'd just received a blow to his stomach. *Lil was raped?* Without another thought, Thomas ran to the tool shed.

"Do you expect me to believe that Thomas took you back believing that we'd had an affair?"

"Yes, I did." Thomas cocked the shotgun and Clay

spun around. When Thomas saw the baby in Clay's arms, he immediately lowered the gun.

"Give the baby to Lillianna now!" Thomas demanded.

"What are you going to do, shoot me for holding *my own* baby?" Clay looked to Lillianna. "Lillianna and I had an agreement. She didn't uphold her end of the bargain so now I'm taking payment."

"For someone who took advantage of a young Amish woman, you have a lot of nerve. Don't think for one minute that you're going to get away with rape *and* kidnapping."

Clay laughed. "You don't know who you're dealing with."

Thomas raised the gun again. "You don't know who *you're* dealing with."

"The baby's going with me."

"Over my dead body," Thomas threatened.

"Clay, please! She didn't do anything wrong," Lillianna cried. "I forgive you, Clay. I forgive you for what you've done to me."

Clay turned around and frowned at Lillianna.

Thomas took the distraction as an opportunity to rescue Mercy from Clay's arms.

"If you sign over your parental rights, we'll consider not pressing charges. I hear rape can carry a life sentence," Thomas bargained. "With fringe benefits."

Clay threw his hands up in surrender. "Fine. Keep the baby."

Several moments later, Clay Stevenson was driving down the road, and out of their lives, for good.

Lillianna melted into Thomas' arms, her body trembling with fear. "I'm so glad you came. I was so scared."

"Shh…you don't need to be frightened anymore. That man is never going to touch you or our baby again," Thomas whispered into her hair. "I'm so sorry, Lil. I had no idea that Clay raped you."

"At first I didn't want to tell you because I didn't want you to stop your treatments. I knew that if I did, you would come home and Clay wouldn't give you the money to continue. I didn't want you to die. After he did it the first time, I knew I couldn't undo what had been done anyway." Tears welled in her eyes. "Oh, Tommy, it was so awful. I tried with all my might to get away…" She broke off, sobbing.

Thomas clenched his fists. *I wish I had killed him.* His frustration mounted. "He did it more than once?"

She nodded. "I'm not sure how many times. Sometimes he would put something into my drink without me knowing."

"I feel so awful that you stayed with that wretched man for *me*, and then when I came back from treatment…" He raked his hands through his hair. "Forgive me, Lil. Forgive me for jumping to conclusions and assuming… What kind of man am I?"

"It's not your fault; you didn't know. I should have said something to you about it, but I was too frightened. When I told Clay I was pregnant, he wanted to force me to have an abortion. I told him that I wouldn't, so he threatened me. He said that if I kept the baby, that he would come and take her and that I would never see her again, if I ever told anybody what happened. He must've assumed I told you."

"What a wicked man. I never would have thought."

"Nobody would have. You'd never know by looking at him. He looks like a nice man." Lillianna shook her head. "It was my fault."

Thomas frowned. "I don't understand. How can you say it's your fault?"

"I wore that dress to the charity auction—"

Thomas' eyes widened. "Wait! Are you saying you think it's *your* fault because of that dress in the paper?"

Lillianna nodded.

Thomas shook his head. "No, Lil. I admit that you looked good in that dress, and compared to Amish apparel I can see how you'd be uncomfortable in it. But there was nothing overly inappropriate about it."

"But Clay said I looked seductive in it."

"You looking nice in an outfit does *not* give Clay the right to force you against your will. I know and agree that sometimes women dress much more immodestly than they should, but not you. You would never dress that way. I saw the dress, Lil." He took a deep breath. "But either way, when he attacked you he was committing a crime. And that is *never* okay. Do you understand?"

She dipped her head slightly.

He raised her chin and their eyes met. "It wasn't your fault, Lil. I don't ever want you to think that. Okay?"

Lillianna nodded.

"I can't believe we just let him go." Thomas felt like running Clay down, pulling out the shotgun, and ending this despicable man's life.

"God will take care of him," Lillianna assured. "But I pray that he will find Jesus."

"Lil, never in a million years could I have found a better woman than you. You are amazing."

"I can't do any less than what Jesus did for me."

Dear Lillianna,

Thank you for your letter. I admit that I almost threw it away without reading it. I'm sorry for the words of anger and judgment that you received in my last letter. I had no idea that Clay forced you. I feel terrible that you came into my home thinking it was a safe place, while my husband took advantage of you. I can't imagine what you must have been feeling.

I think it's commendable that you are not pressing charges. However, I intend to. A man, especially a man who is supposed to be a leader, should never be able to get away with a crime. If he is not punished, he will think that he can do it again. Therefore, I intend to pros-

ecute him. *Don't be surprised if you receive a subpoena in the mail.*

I'm happy to hear that you and Thomas have reconciled. Congratulations on your marriage.
God bless you,
Candace

Epilogue

Thomas strolled up behind Lillianna and placed his hands over her expanding belly. He pressed his warm lips to her neck, causing shivers to dance up her spine.

"What do you say, if we have a girl, we name her Grace?" Tommy proposed.

Lillianna turned around and melted into his arms. "Mercy and Grace. I like it. But what if the baby's a boy?"

Thomas shrugged. "Thomas, Jr.?"

Lillianna laughed. "Maybe we can search for a male name that means grace."

"We could call him Jishikamiku." Thomas raised his eyebrows.

Lillianna gave him an amused grin.

"Hey, that's his ninja name. It's sort of cool, isn't it?" Thomas chuckled.

Lillianna shook her head. "I think Thomas, Jr. will be just fine."

Thomas pulled her by the hand to the sofa and they sat down. Mercy, who sat on the floor with a few toys surrounding her, stood up and toddled toward them. Lillianna picked her up and set her between them.

Thomas picked up the newspaper. "You know, Lil, I'm all for mercy and grace, but I can't deny that this gives me a sense of satisfaction."

Lillianna read the headline again: *Congressman Behind Bars*. She sighed and admitted to herself that she, too, felt a sense of justice. "Perhaps that is what it will take for him to find Jesus, *jah*?"

"I have no doubt that you will continue to pray for him."

"We've done a lot of things wrong and God gave us a second chance. How can we not wish Clay get the same opportunity?"

"You're right. God has definitely blessed me with more than I could ever hope for." Thomas picked up Mercy. "We should get ready for meeting now. If we're late again, Jonathan will give me a hard time."

Lillianna leaned over and placed a tantalizing kiss on his lips. "Let's give him something to talk about."

* * * * *

A Special Thank You

I'd like to take this time to thank everyone that had any involvement in this book and its production, including Marla at the Mexican clinics, Mom and Dad, who have always been supportive of my writing, my long-suffering Family—especially my handsome, encouraging Hubby—my former-Amish friends who have helped immensely in my understanding of the Amish ways, my supportive Pastor and Church family, my Proofreaders, my Editor, my CIA Facebook friends who have been a tremendous help, my wonderful Readers who buy, read, and leave encouraging reviews and emails, my awesome Street Team who, I'm confident, will "Sprede the Word" about my books! And last, but certainly not least, I'd like to thank my Precious LORD and SAVIOUR JESUS CHRIST, for without Him, none of this would have been possible!

Get 4 FREE REWARDS!

We'll send you 2 FREE Books plus 2 FREE Mystery Gifts.

Love Inspired® Suspense books feature Christian characters facing challenges to their faith... and lives.

FREE Value Over $20

HOME *on the* RANCH

YES! Please send me the **Home on the Ranch Collection** in Larger Print. This collection begins with 3 FREE books and 2 FREE gifts in the first shipment. Along with my 3 free books, I'll also get the next 4 books from the Home on the Ranch Collection, in LARGER PRINT, which I may either return and owe nothing, or keep for the low price of $5.24 U.S./ $5.89 CDN each plus $2.99 for shipping and handling per shipment*. If I decide to continue, about once a month for 8 months I will get 6 or 7 more books, but will only need to pay for 4. That means 2 or 3 books in every shipment will be FREE! If I decide to keep the entire collection, I'll have paid for only 32 books because 19 books are FREE! I understand that accepting the 3 free books and gifts places me under no obligation to buy anything. I can always return a shipment and cancel at any time. My free books and gifts are mine to keep no matter what I decide.

268 HCN 3760 468 HCN 3760

Name	(PLEASE PRINT)	
Address		Apt. #
City	State/Prov.	Zip/Postal Code

Signature (if under 18, a parent or guardian must sign)

Mail to the **Reader Service:**

IN U.S.A.: P.O. Box 1341, Buffalo, New York 14240-8531
IN CANADA: P.O. Box 603, Fort Erie, Ontario L2A 5X3

* Terms and prices subject to change without notice. Prices do not include applicable taxes. Sales tax applicable in NY. Canadian residents will be charged applicable taxes. This offer is limited to one order per household. All orders subject to approval. Credit or debit balances in a customer's account(s) may be offset by any other outstanding balance owed by or to the customer. Please allow 3 to 4 weeks for delivery. Offer available while quantities last. Offer not available to Quebec residents.